THE SECRET ISLANDS

BY THE SAME AUTHOR

Watchers at the Pond (1962) • *Argen the Gull (1964)*

FRANKLIN RUSSELL

The Secret Islands

With photographs by the author

W · W · NORTON & COMPANY · INC · NEW YORK

To JACQUELINE *and* MICHAEL

Contents

Photographs between pages 130 and 131

THE SECRET ISLANDS

1

To the Islands

INSIDE THE ISLAND, a million birds sleep. The forest and grass conceal them and drip with the moisture of a night-borne mist. The gulls are silent and face toward invisible Greenland and a horizon of transparent, shifting colors. The sun shows its lip; light the color of blood runs across the sea and strikes into the spruces.

WHEN I AM DROWSY and ready to sleep in my apartment in Manhattan, I think of the island. It rests in a part of the mind where its smells, colors, and sounds, its hoary rocks and hordes of creatures, can be transformed instantly into an image in my eye. I see it under a cool sun as its day ends and night flows from the sea. But the island does not sleep; instead, it awakens. The opaque air streams with exquisite patterns and structures of sound which climb almost visibly from my watching eyes. As though in echo, the body of the island quivers with music. It is a *singing* island, and the earth soughs with longing. I sleep with the sound of its song in my ears.

The singing island is magnetic; it draws me back in

memory. It implies the revelation of a universal secret. But the secret is elusive. Perhaps it is in myself.

I can see another island. A vandal horde of creatures stands together, shoulder to shoulder, stretching out of sight. They watch me and their voices are Niagara at the bottom of its fall. I turn into the wind and the stench of death seizes my throat.

The islands shuttle in and out of memory. I sleep, dream, see an island sitting like a castle and its creatures rise from the battlements like clouds of arrows. I dream of an island where the light is silver and the air is filled with expectation; an army of birds lands on a light-speckled sea and instantly they become submarines in search of food.

The islands insist on an evocation of atmosphere. How can I describe them? Poetically? Musically? But no poetry or music can communicate as well as those voices singing from the earth; if I can describe *them*, I can evoke the islands.

I had lived in cities for fifteen years, and I was stifled by the synthetic nature of life. Nobody prevented me from leaving the city, so the fifteen years were my responsibility. But I had walked for too long against the flow of people. I had become accustomed to the city and its perversions: dog-defiled streets and people-defiled parks. The good things about the city were less easy to remember than before. I had become doubtful, compressed, and wary, and I needed more than a few lungfuls of country air to rejuvenate me. I was thirty-six

years of age, life half done, and I wanted affirmation of
an older order of life, before the megalopolis.

Accordingly, I stepped into an automobile and drove
north from New York City in an effort to refresh my
memory of the natural world. At the same time, I understood I would be in a void, traveling in space and time,
and unencumbered by the harness of responsible city
life: rent, insurance, friends, fear.

As I drove, I realized that I was executing an impulse
of civilized man. I was escaping. I was heading for a
desert island, a cabin in the woods, a solitary explora-
tion, and so I was a special man. I had been surprised at
how many friends, half-aware of what I planned to do,
had suggested they come with me. One man had called
and said, "I've got six weeks off and I could carry some
of your stuff." None of them really knew where I was
going or why, but they understood absolutely the
significance of the journey.

In that respect, they were wiser than I. I had little
concept of anything except the need to go. I did not
anticipate how constant exposure to natural phenomena
would provide a new view of world and self. Once there,
everything was to become piercingly real. I awakened
in a forest and looked into the eyes of a northern jay
standing on my chest, and I swear there was communication between us. Now, what sort of nonsense is that?
In times of solitude, alone on a scrap of rock far offshore, or lost in tundralike peatlands, I could not
visualize the city or my previous life at all. I forgot the

names of close friends. Was I mad? Once, standing on
the top of cliffs which overlooked a sea of polished
obsidian, I was convinced that in the next second I
would see into the future. My eyes searched the horizon.
A mute and awesome sun rose, and its silent enlarge-
ment changed me. How? I cannot say. But each day
thereafter carried a memory of it.

One thing I did understand as I left the city: I was
heading for islands—granite islands, earthen islands,
forested islands, uninhabited islands and islands over-
flowing with life. I understood that a man born on an
island, the South Island of New Zealand, as I was, is
not the same as continental man. There is always an
expanse of sea separating him from the rest of the world.
If he leaves the island, he leaves the safe place of his
fondest feelings. He may resolve his unease by scorning
his birthplace or by reviling the sea, but he will remain
haunted by the memory of his island home.

What sets him apart from mainland men is that by
leaving the island, he overcomes his fear of the mainland mass. As long as he lives in his parochial island
world, he feels secure; the sea deters his escape but it
also keeps him safe from invasion. He knows his world,
but the mainland is vast and unknowable. Yet he goes.
Why?

Perhaps the answer is in the island itself, the place
of dreams and reverie. Is it possible to live there, or
must the island be denied? No answer. The island marks
the horizon in azure isolation, enchanted for a Meredith

or a Milton, and proffers the realization of fantasy: nubile women, bountiful fruit, gentle winds and sun. It suggests escape, and we go there to paint, or to die, or to escape our oppressors.

It is the same for animals. The island draws them too. Early in my journey, I was at sea in a spring storm and saw a flock of birds being swept along the trough of a wave, barely visible in the spumed air. They were gannets, and I knew that despite the ferocity of the storm, they were heading for an island I was to visit. I lay on the deck of a pitching fishing boat and saw a score of lithe black petrels walking daintily on the water. It was late afternoon and suddenly they all turned, as though identically animated, and flew north. They were heading toward another island, where I would meet them again.

The island, any island, may be buried in the body of a storm, lost in mist, or caught in ice, but the birds will find it. Some travel up to ten thousand miles to find a burrow three inches wide, buried in a spruce jungle. The island is the only place on earth where they can breed; this makes all storms, distances, and natural disasters insignificant. They *must* return to the island.

As I drove through New England, the night air querulous with spring frogs, I knew I would outdrive the American spring and meet late-winter snow and ice as I reached into maritime Canada. There would be the islands and the beginning of the fantasy.

My feeling about islands is not normal. My first sight

of an island is followed immediately by an urge to land on it. I was a scout cub on patrol in English woodlands when I came on a small mere. A tiny island stood in its center. One look at it and I was galvanized. To the accompaniment of derisive comments from the other cubs, I stripped off my clothes and swam to the island, landed, and shivered in the autumnal chill. I looked at the mainland and its knot of cubs and laughed. I was on the island and they were not.

The size of the island is not important. It can be as big as Tasmania or as small as an islet in the Delaware River. Beauty does not seem to matter. I get much the same feeling from the purple hills of Papeete as I do from the gray sobriety of Heligoland.

There is a word for all this: islomania. It was coined by Lawrence Durrell, who suffers, *revels,* rather, in his affliction. Islomania is revealed in many ways, from Durrell's own sinuous elegance of expression about Aegean islands, to the simple statement of a Newfoundland friend of mine, Tom Stockley, who stamped on the ground and said, "I just don't feel right till I got this island earth underfoot."

Fishermen are special victims of islomania. They look with wonder and respect at all islands, not only because they represent anchorage and shelter, or are located in good fishing areas, but because there is something mystic about them. I once met an old fisherman who said, as we approached a tiny island, "I wish I were landin' on her for the *first* time."

Islomania stimulates the imagination and sends it ranging to islands not yet visited or into times other than the present.

I drove north among squabbling robins and saw flowers at the edge of forests, but I was not thinking about them. My mind went roving into the past . . .

Captain James Cook stands on a beach in the Sandwich Islands, flanked by his lieutenants and seamen. He has spent the greater part of his life searching for islands, and this is as far as he has ever traveled. It is a brilliant clear day, the air warm and dry. The *Resolution*, mainsails and topsails furled, floats motionless in the bay. The curl of each tiny wave along the beach sparkles with tropical intensity, then dies. In slow and stately motion, an islander steps out from the palm trees, raises a spear and drives it through Cook's chest.

New Hampshire flicked past.

The soil of Mauritius is red in my dreaming imagination. Bees and bright flowers glint in the lush vegetation. A man with a dog pushes through long grasses at the edge of a marsh. Ahead, a big gooselike bird, flightless and clumsy because it knows nothing except this one island, tries to flee. The dog rushes forward. In a moment, the last dodo on earth is dead.

Rain, thunder, the whine of tires on a turnpike.

I am on another island, and the air is menacing with the suggestion of death. A dozen men move through massed thousands of great auks, as big as geese, black and white and flightless. The great auks have been made helpless by their island. They swam to it,

massed on it to breed, and their sheer numbers intimidated all predators, except this last one. Methodically, the men slam short wooden boards down on the
birds' heads, while behind them other men pitchfork
the birds into big piles. On a distant ridge, more men
tend cauldrons and fires to boil down the fat of the
birds. The men feed carcasses of the birds into the
flames. The bodies are fat and burn brightly. I see
myself reach down to scoop up handfuls of the bones
of great auks, butchered two hundred years before my
visit.

The Maine woods, cloaked in fog, raced past my
window.

I approach an island little more than an acre in size.
It is almost covered with walruses, stiffly intent as they
watch the ship. They look defenseless, and they are.
Like the great auks, they had known the island to be
complete protection against their enemies. My eye is
quickly filled with their jowls and whiskers and white
tusks. A spasm of fright sends them wriggling for
safety, and they hurl themselves on top of each other,
churn the water, bark, cough, and groan. My ship
moves forward pitilessly and the human eye sates
itself on the frenzy of the animals.

The Maine fog cleared and the sea appeared.

I am on a very large island. A tui sings in a kahikatea
tree, and before me, on his knees, is a man brushing
earth away from a partially shattered egg, almost as
big as a soup plate. It is half-buried in the soil, the
egg of the legendary moa, extinct for several hundred
years. The moa, twelve feet high and flightless, had
made this island its own until a mysterious race of

men, the Morioris, came. They ate the moa. Then came the Maoris and they ate the Morioris.

I left Maine and crossed a bridge to Campobello Island, where the journey began.

I had one summer to do this trip; therefore, I would have to see with a special vision. I needed Mowgli's sight, and the conviction that, like the hunter's, my life depended on seeing well. I wanted to penetrate chaos and put some truth into the meaningless mixture of sea, shore, bird, and man. Was I being presumptuous to think that I could truly see after years of looking at the city?

I wanted the leisure and freedom to contemplate the meaning of the physical earth: its colors and shadows, the patterns of its leaves, the cries of birds, and the shape of flight silhouetted against pacific light. There was a natural order of things, I knew, or else the sky would be black, the sea purple, and all birds yellow.

I sailed from a small fishing town. Herring gulls decorated a foreshore, and two whales showed gleaming, curved backs. I looked at my fellow travelers, but they saw nothing. I looked at the village, but it was blind. I turned with the boat, alone in space. I could see; or could I?

The islands I was to visit are priceless monuments of primeval earth, only a couple of days from New York. Nothing can touch them; no hot-dog stands or cola bottles, cigarette butts or bottle tops.

The southernmost island is a faint mark, an echo, in

thick Bay of Fundy mist. Hay Island is a scrap of nearly
flat land, half-clad in forest, half-grassed, and girdled
with rocks and shingly beaches. You may circle it in a
boat and see gulls standing in serried lines along its
shore and know nothing about it. Its grasslands, once
farmed by primitive people, conceal thousands of nesting eider ducks, so thickly placed that you cannot walk
among them without crushing eggs. If you are very, very
lucky, you may see the ducks make their run for the sea.

The next island is Hay Island's big neighbor, Kent
Island, which is fewer than a thousand feet away, and
equally undistinguished. It is the same mix of forest,
rock, grass, and shingle, and it would be uninteresting
to anyone but an islomaniac, except for one thing. It lies
athwart the mouth of the Passamaquoddy herring territory. This has made Kent Island the greatest herring-
gull colony in North America. A susurration of gull cries
pours out of the mist, and I shiver at the memory.

The third island, four hundred miles north, is the
antithesis of Kent Island. I see it sprawled offshore from
a tiny Quebec resort town, Percé. Bonaventure Island
is fewer than five hundred acres in area, and is haphazardly settled, its half dozen houses dropped like
afterthoughts along the fringe of spruce forest that
covers most of it. Progress, civilization, enlightenment,
have entirely missed Bonaventure. Its handful of human
beings exist in uncaring detachment on the mainland
side of the island. More than two hundred thousand
birds live in uproarious activity on the seaward side. In

between the two, it is possible to understand the nature of solitude.

The fourth island is a study in ultimates. It is the loneliest, the least accessible, the most fascinating and repellent. Funk Island is a chunk of granite dropped in the middle of the Labrador Current forty miles off the northeast coast of Newfoundland. My first sight of it is a view of nothing. It is dull, flat, treeless. Yet this bleak rock is a natural-history monument; the great auk made its last stand here in the western Atlantic and was wiped out. It contains one of the world's greatest colonies of murres, a type of sea bird. More than a million murres are packed into a few acres. It is a spectacle powerful enough to numb the senses and create lasting disbelief. I look and see the air above the island move blackly with flying figures.

The fifth island appears, momentarily forbidding in the gray tints of predawn light. Its peaks look definitely Tahitian as my boat bucks toward it against a heavy Atlantic swell. Even at a distance, Great Island's special place among the islands is apparent. My dancing glass picks out thousands of watching puffins lining the cliffs of the island. They are humorless, homuncular soldiers, dressed in immaculate accoutrements, who have, with indefatigable burrowing ability, riddled the interior of the island like a sponge. Great Island is two miles off the southeast coast of Newfoundland and a little more than a thousand miles from New York.

From a peak on Great Island, arctic air touching my

forehead, I see Green Island, a sea-bird bastion if ever there was one. It rises a hundred feet out of the sea, a Norman castle of rock, moated in salt water. With my glass on it, I see it is tiered with sea birds. They line its cliffs like knights; an alarm, and they blossom upward.

Beyond Green is yet another island. It is withdrawn, oddly quiet after the uproar of birds on the other islands. It is called Gull Island, but few gulls use it. It is really Mother Carey's Island; her children live there during the northern summer. More than a million of them have drilled the earth of the island to create an underground colony. Each night, hundreds of thousands of them come to the island from the deep ocean, and for a few mad hours, dance and cavort and sing to each other. Like midnight musicians, they transform the island, but at dawn they are gone. Pierced by my glass in daylight, Gull Island is nothing, a blob of matter stolidly fixed in the sea.

The last island is scarcely an island at all, at least by comparison with these miniature cities of birds. It is Newfoundland, a place of the man-islander. When I left New York, I had equated escape with relief from human beings. Instead, I discovered men who were scarcely touched by this century, who personified symbolic escape. Through their eyes, I saw other centuries. With them, I practiced older arts of living. Once, caught on the deep sea in a tiny boat in a storm, one of them bellowed at me: "Does ye think we'll make it?" and while I pondered this, he laughed and laughed. I passed into a world of vivid memories. An old woman, by the power of her narrative and imagination, made her husband, dead fifty years, appear in his sea clothes at the end of her porch. I rowed with men whose arthritic fingers were bent to the shape of an oar handle, and met Lolita, or her sister, and went to a village of mad children. I caught the codfish, and turned their drying bodies on racks, and swam in the Labrador Current, and crammed into forecastles filled with snoring men, and ate moose and cloudberries and eider ducks. I made sentimental journeys with old fishermen back to the islands of their birth, and on one island, Flowers, became a kind of archaeologist to discover a long-dead community. I traveled toward self-knowledge but the journey was circular.

Inside the traveling were buried the minute details that collectively created the truth I sought. A fox, unaware of my eye, leaped at the edge of a cliff and caught a bird in mid-air. An eider duck, immobile, six inches from my boot, moved slightly to allow a duckling to dig under her breast feathers, and I could see the question in her eyes. Young gulls with broken wings watched me doubtfully and showed their hurt and confusion at the storm that had crippled them. A group of trees clung together, dimmed and softened by a touch of mist. An ochreous island appeared, held in a sea of pacific red. I saw everything anew: pastel sunsets, a city of icebergs, a hovering eagle, and felt a Nordic chill. A brahmsian shoreline swept into a sea glittering with gold. Corruption underfoot and a sinister rush of wings. I lay half asleep under a velvet sky, heard the sound of Mars and felt scintillations from Mercury. Eventually, I knew something. Wilderness man was in touch with the mainspring of human effort and inspiration: the kinetic energy of earth.

I face an island. This is the divisive moment. Before it, I am in the predictable world of the mainland. After it, I am isolated, probably alone. The landings may be dangerous because many of the islands have steep, rocky shore lines which resist invasion in all but the calmest weather. Each landing leaves me with my breath caught in my throat and looking with relief at unbroken limbs. At the moment of landing, the boat rises and falls six or seven feet in the swell. I am balanced in the bows. Confronting me is a mass of slippery rocks, steep, jagged and glistening. My boatman is tense. A slight misjudgment can wreck his livelihood and put us both in the cold water.

I jump. I know the jump is nothing. My intellect tells me I can easily leap four feet; my imagination tells me I will be crushed against rock if I fall. I land asprawl, and my pack cants me over while one foot sinks into the water. Over my shoulder, I see the heavy boat falling. Its blunt stem will grind the rocks. Fingernails break; an ankle moves away and I am wholly on the island.

The danger of an island landing is one thing; the uncertainty of even getting a chance to land is another. Waiting to reach each island becomes an agony of time, of still, hollow days while I lie with mist in my lungs and endless swelling waves in my imagination. When will the boatman come? Is that the sound of his engine? Will the wind change?

At last I awake in the middle of the night with the wind hissing in the trees and, far distant, the sea roaring. There is an edge of desperation here, compounded of days fleeting by out of control, of one brief summer, of the knowledge that I am a mainlander now, at the mercy of the beckoning islands.

2

The Running Eiders

AN ISLAND is a place of refuge for men and animals; its isolation slows the insistent thrust of time. For a moment, as I stand on the highest part of the island, sea water all around me, I believe I am immortal. Nothing can reach me here. I touch rough bark, feel the scrunch of stones underfoot, look into silent pools, and hear the sound of the sea and of my own heart.

Then I laugh because it is all a delusion.

The fact is, an island may have to be deserted. Life can be affirmed only by the denial of its security; this is as true for animals as it is for men. Hay Island, ten miles from Grand Manan, is a monument to this. Men have long gone from it, and their remains suggest how illusory was the security of their island. No one has lived on Hay Island for many years. Two abandoned houses, walls sagging and windows empty, are littered with the debris of another century; they are the decaying nests of extinct creatures.

There are no ghosts on Hay, no flicker of spirits in the presence of the artifacts. A grocery bill from the 1800's evokes nothing. Nail holes in the walls, a black fingerprint on a board, the name *Anne* carved on a joist, none of these things suggest human occupancy. Perhaps this is because Hay Island is retrogressing, going back to an earlier millennium under the stimulus of a really enduring form of life: ducks.

In the prime of man's occupancy of the island, beginning in the eighteenth century, he decimated the eider ducks. He pillaged their nests for the eggs, which are delicious, and for the valuable eider down. Now, the men have gone, protective laws are in force, and the eider ducks of Hay Island are making their comeback.

This was the southernmost island on my summer trip, the easiest to reach, and it had special significance for me. For years, I had heard stories of how the eiders were taking over the island. Two years before, I had made a quick trip into the area, but the Grand Mananers, residents of a large island nearby, had said, "You're too early. The ducks aren't leaving yet." The next year, I had tried again, to be told, "You're too late. The ducks have gone."

I knew my entire summer could be plagued by such uncertainties, might even turn into a disaster. Therefore, after landing on Grand Manan and waiting for several days while a heavy sea subsided, I was very anxious. It was one thing to sit comfortably in a New York City apartment and compute duck habits, quite another thing to be a prisoner behind surf roaring along an island shoreline.

Anxiety increased when my boat eventually eased

me cautiously through mist to reach Hay Island one late afternoon. The tide was down and the boatman was fearful of hidden shoals. "Very dangerous at low tide," he muttered. "I shouldn't have brought you." He anchored, unshipped the dinghy and began rowing me through shallowing water. Abruptly the mist lifted and I had a Neptunian view of Hay Island. We were well below it, so great is the fall of the Fundy tide, and it looked as though the island had suffered a calamity; the sea had been drained from it.

"Good luck," said the boatman. "I'll be back in two tides."

My boots squelched among thick, lank weeds. The sun appeared, ten of its diameters from the horizon and its passage veiled by hurdles of clouds. I felt the urgency of its fall and quickened my pace up an embankment of stones that surrounds the island and protects it from the sea.

"You're too late. The ducks have gone."

I rounded the curve of the shore, trees, shrubs and ponds on my left, sunset on my right. The shore was luminous from the sunlight now filtered through orange, red and pink clouds. It was a spectacle but not what I sought. I walked and faced down the long western shore of the island. With the tide out, it was a grand sweep of shingle pouring into the withdrawn sea. As far as I could see, eider ducks walked toward the water. They hobbled and tripped on stones; those nearest to me skittered and fell in their haste. Each duck led a small, compact group of ducklings. I had arrived in time to see the eider ducks deserting the island with their new families. The eiders make their run to the sea, usually at dusk, as soon as the ducklings are strong enough to walk well. In the nest, concealed under a mother's breast or a covering of feathers, the ducklings are reasonably safe. In the water, capable of diving from predators, they have a fair chance of survival. But walking on land before they can fly, they are terribly vulnerable. This gives their passage from the nest to the sea a peculiar and touching urgency.

Forty ducks were in sight at once, all leading ducklings. I paused, watched, then walked forward into the world of the running eiders.

The ducks were Lilliputians on the shingled barrier to the sea. Behind them lay scrub, long grass and spruce where they had brooded their eggs. Ahead of them lay the sun; easy to imagine it was their beacon. Ducks floated inshore, a communal body which certainly drew the running ducks on; I could see family groups, already in the water, swimming rapidly toward the main group.

As I walked, I was subject to multilayered sensation. My eyes moved back and forth but I knew I was always missing something. I walked high on the shore to avoid cutting off the seagoing families. If I scared ducks from their families, they left the ducklings in the refuge of the shore grasses.

But my feet crashing on the stones generated a general alarm and ducks which had not yet hatched their families began to flee. The first duck was a blur in my

eye and a rush of wind in my face, so close did she fly
past me. She had fled at the last moment, only when
she was sure that I would stumble over her nest. Her
flight set the tempo. Ducks came out of the grass and
shrub like missiles. Each time harsh clatter of wings
beat through dead sticks, a crash of heavy body flung
through the undergrowth, then the sleek, speedy body
of the duck appeared, eyes bright as she appraised the
intruder, the sunset, and her path of escape.

I walked a hundred paces, fascinated, almost willing
to be cut down by the ducks, now coming out of the
undergrowth by the score. Many of them collided in
mid-air; twice, they flew directly at me, blind to me
specifically, but unnerving at high speed. Each duck
saw me a moment before collision. Wings splayed
desperately, tails fanned, and I was enveloped in a gale
of ruptured air.

The sun glowed and threw out profuse color. I
became ultrasensitive. Demonstrably, I was the only
man experiencing this place and time; such a peak of
awareness, exhilarant and tingling, might not come to
me again. At the same time, it was frightening to be so
close to the reality of wild lives, like taking a front-row
seat at a boxing match and realizing, for the first time,
the ferocious power of the blows.

The sea-run was at its peak. The shore swarmed with
duck families. In the sea, back-lit by a dying sun, the
offshore ducks had withdrawn slightly in deference to
my presence. A score of duck families hurried across the

intervening water. For the ducklings, the relief of being in the water was enormous. They dived, flapped stubby wings, shook themselves, skittered around their mothers in tight, excited circles. Then, the family groups set out, big ships followed by lines of small tenders, toward the waiting presence of the main duck flock.

For a moment, I was happy to watch; but such was the insistence of the sea-run to express itself that I could not remain an observer. A concerned quack behind me warned that a duck was close. I turned and saw a duck and ducklings at the edge of the undergrowth. She was in a quandary, the decision to head for the sea already made, the nest deserted, the undergrowth navigated, only to find an enemy barring her path. For a moment, we watched each other in a common comprehension of the situation. Then, she made her choice, launched herself suddenly and flew past me. The dilemma was transferred to the eight ducklings who met my gaze, as baffled as their mother had been a moment before. Their urge to reach the sea was irresistible. To turn back was impossible. Their hesitation was neither fear nor doubt, merely consideration of their chances of getting *past* me.

They made their run in a group, stomping across the rocks like a phalanx of tiny Martians, as if the impetus of their miniature charge could sweep me out of the way. I stepped back and they were were underfoot. I tried to stop one with my boot but he hurdled it in a sprawl of paddles and stub wings. I ran around them and tried to stop them again, drive them back into the shelter of the grass. Impossible. The run for the sea was manic. Their anxiety was so great they knocked each other down, jostled and blundered. Yet despite interposing stones and debris, they stuck together all the way.

I watched them move down the shingle and hit the water. Almost immediately, a duck flew over their heads, calling. As one creature, the ducklings dived. One second, eight tiny forms bobbed; the next instant, eight circles of displaced water expanded. The ducklings reappeared fifty feet offshore; the duck landed and led her family quickly away.

Until this moment, I thought I had been seeing the full scope of events; but with slow-rising horror, I saw what was *really* happening along this shore. I had observed gulls everywhere, but on offshore islands they are omnipresent and almost unnoticed.

A duck appeared out of the undergrowth, about a hundred yards away. She led a straggle of fifteen ducklings, probably a coalition of two families. One duckling, smaller than the rest, trailed by six inches, and that was enough. A gull plucked him aloft, his fall and rise so swift it looked like one clean movement. The big bird passed over my head and choked the duckling down audibly as he flew. The remaining ducklings spurted into a more compact mass. The searun did not waver. The hovering, gliding gulls, so apparently casual, so outwardly benign, were everywhere, awaiting a chance for a duckling. The running eiders were neither comic nor touching; they were involved in a mathematical experiment in survival.

The equation was simple. Any duckling, on land or on water, who lagged more than five or six inches from his fellows, was killed immediately. The gulls twisted down, beaks agape and paddle feet lowered, struck stone or water, and rebounded buoyantly with their quarry. The ducks were unconcerned at the loss of the ducklings and did not even flinch as the gulls came down. Their presence was, apparently, anticipated, an historic fact of the sea-run. Even when gulls struck so close to the family group that their outflung wings swept the air above the ducks' heads, they provoked no threatening move, no quack of fear or rage. The ducks kept leading their broods, erect-necked and watchful, toward the haven of the water.

The sun disappeared with a final flourish; the run for the sea was thinning. Fewer than a score of ducks were visible. I walked down to the water's edge and looked back toward the heart of the island. The fringe of grass, the undergrowth and spruces, were washed with soft light. At that moment, one last duck appeared among the grasses and headed toward me as though I did not exist. Midway down the gravel, she saw me, turned diagonally, and revealed her family. It was enormous, more than twenty nestlings; probably she had picked up two other families of ducklings who had been temporarily deserted by their mothers. She watched me closely, made no attempt to fly, then hit the water with her big family and fled offshore. The tiny birds showed their elbowed paddle legs as they swam rapidly to keep up with her.

I took one last look up the shore, and as if I had summoned him, a lone duckling appeared. He stood motionless, facing two hundred feet of cruelly stoned beach, himself only hours out of the egg, the light of the sunken sun blinding his new eyes, alone. But he had no doubts. To the sea! He began his run.

At the same instant, a passing gull turned to investigate, apparently puzzled that any duckling could be *alone* on this beach. As he hovered, I hurled a stone and the gull veered away. Another gull took his position. I hurled more stones and the duckling stumbled downhill to the clatter of falling stones and the inquiring *kaa*'s of the watchful gulls.

Even as I threw the stones, I knew that alone, the duckling was doomed. I must catch him and try to find a way to see him safely into the custody of his family. He zigzagged, fell, rolled, ran into my waiting hand. A gull hovered overhead, lit cold as steel in the moldering light. I remembered how wood ducklings could jump and fall a hundred feet to the ground without injury. Most young sea birds can fall from steep cliffs, smash onto rocks, and swim away unharmed. I decided to take a risk.

By this time, the conglomerate duck family was fully a hundred and fifty feet offshore. I hurled the duckling with all my strength at the sunset. He turned over and over silently, a splay of wing stubs and tiny paddle feet, and hit the water. Immediately, a gull was there. But the duckling whisked under water; the gull hovered, watching. The duckling appeared but went down again before the gull could move toward him.

Finally, a long underwater swim brought the youngster up at the flank of the big family. He shot among them and disappeared.

The desertion of the island was a hint, a clue. I looked forward into the summer and wondered what else I might know. How much would these islands tell me about my own life?

The ducks withdrew and were lost in dusk; I sat till it was dark and contemplated life's urge to have its way and to survive.

3

The Devil's Driveway

THE SUMMER LIGHT of Newfoundland is gentle but piercing. It implies the arctic and indicates how the island is caught midway between two extremes; pole and equator. This was the centerpiece of my traveling. From Newfoundland I would jump outward to smaller islands. On it, I would meet my first islanders, men whose lives had been directed by their separation from the mainland.

I landed on Newfoundland in July, and snow clung to distant lines of low hills. The road stretched before me through bulges of bare, gray-green doughnut hills. The rocks and black heathlands on either side of me seemed only recently freed of ice. I did not know it, but I was on the Devil's Driveway, the island's main road, a Frankenstein creation that interposed itself between me and my goal.

The road turns in a half-moon across the heart of Newfoundland, beginning at Port aux Basques, where I had landed from a car ferry, and ending on the southeast coast at the island's capital, St. John's. It is a pity, in my mind, that in the mid-nineteen sixties the road was tamed, paved, straightened and fitted with picnic tables. When I first drove it, nothing encouraged the traveler to press on to his destination. The driveway discouraged tourists, but it also gave Newfoundland a flavor of its own. The highway said damnation to foreigners: come to this island at your own risk; you are not welcome. I saw a car with front *and* back windows punctured by a single stone. I met a woman driver whose foot was bleeding because a stone had penetrated the steel floor of her car, the carpet, *and* her thick leather sole.

The Devil's Driveway was merciless to all automobiles. Foreign cars, vaunted for durability, fell apart even more quickly than domestic U.S. cars. The most vulnerable machines turned out to be ostensibly rugged cross-country vehicles with hard suspensions. If the automobile survived the potholes, corrugations, washouts, and areas under construction, it still faced the pungent possibilities of collision with wandering moose, caribou, sheep, goats, cows, and horses.

But on this bright July morning, as I swung through sleek hills and headed inland, the highway was black and smooth as glass. It was built to what is known locally as "trans-Canada specifications," those of the extremely fast, two-lane road that now crosses the continent from coast to coast. I rushed past still ponds which transmitted flying pictures of snow, and my speed climbed to seventy. The end of the idyll was sudden.

I rounded a curve, and the blacktop ended abruptly. White gravel began. At first, the new surface was a dull throb of sound from jittering wheels, but gradually the road became Dantesque. A curtain of dust particles moved sluggishly between me and the windshield. A car ahead of me threw up an explosion of dust into which I drove grimly, seeing its taillights, six red eyes, gleaming from time to time. Quadrilights glared suddenly as trucks roared past, ten feet high with gravel; metal clanged as stones struck the car.

Each second, I expected the dust to end. But an hour passed; I had a near escape when a stalled dump truck squatted in the middle of the road and I skidded away from it. I seemed to have lost all contact with the normal world. The dust would have to end immediately. I insisted on it. Another hour passed, and my nerve ends became pinpoints of agony as I glared into the stuff boiling away behind a car ahead.

Later, I was to hear stories about the effect of the Driveway. It induced a stupor which sapped the driver's will. In the end, many motorists pulled to the side of the road, where they sat stunned and disbelieving. Hardier fellows got out of their smoking cars and walked through forest and marsh to regain their composure. If he was tough enough to keep driving, the driver felt the need to scream himself weak, give up, let the wheel go, and slump back in the seat.

The hammering road prepared me for any new horror, although scarcely for anything so prosaic as a hitchhiker. He stood beside the road, so well buried in dust that I almost ran him down. He looked just like any other hitchhiker, which was surprising. Somehow, I expected a special kind of hitchhiker, space-suited, perhaps, oxygen tanks on his back.

I would not have stopped, true to the tradition of my suspicious city world where any man without an automobile is a thief and a vagrant, but Newfoundland was, after all, an island, and its people were islanders. I stopped.

The man was tall and thin; his body stooped slightly in the effort to hold himself erect. His pale face looked tubercular and ill (a common sight in Newfoundland), and he slid into the seat with a smile. "Thank you, sir."

Was he going far?

"Just a little way up the drive, thank you."

We pushed on through the dust which covered the instrument panel, seats, floor, and even the inside of the windshield. I started the ventilating fan and cyclones of dust billowed in the car. Covertly, I watched the man. His tapered fingers, cut and ripped by manual work, were flexing slowly in his lap. We plowed through five miles of deep sand that would have stalled us had I stopped. Mercifully, the gravel road ended. The man was silent as we hummed over three miles of blacktop. The radio, released from competition with road noises, asserted itself and played hillbilly music, interspersed with personal messages from Newfoundlanders who lived beyond the reach of telephone.

Bill will be back Monday. Please feed the pigeons. Aunt Mabel sends her love.

The blacktop ended and the road plunged into a
stretch of craters, some of them so big that the bottom
of the car struck rock as we pitched into them. It was a
hard road, the hitchhiker observed unexpectedly. Yes,
it was. I noticed that his left forearm was bent and the
fingers of the hand misshapen. Had he been wounded
in the war? Puzzled, he looked at me and then understood. Oh no, nothing like that. He had broken his arm
when he was a youngster.

For the next five minutes, conversation was impossible as I drove over teeth-shaking corrugations. The
hitchhiker ignored the uproar until the car slewed into
sand again. So I didn't know very much about Newfoundland, eh? Well, not much. Hmm. Things were
different from where I came from. Yes, clearly. But he
wanted to explain the scope of the difference, not have
me assume it.

He had broken his arm when he was a kid living in
an outport, one of a number of isolated fishing villages
which dot the island's coast. There was no doctor within
two hundred miles, and the arm set itself, crooked, of
course. When he had reached a doctor, the arm was
broken again and reset. But the doctor was incompetent
and set it crooked, worse than the original set of the
fracture.

*Martha taken to hospital. Due for exploratory tests
Monday. Keep your fingers crossed. How are Albert and
Joe? Much love.*

The hillbilly music resumed. Yes, it had happened in

an outport. His father had been a fisherman, a dory fisherman. He used to row out of the village every morning at three o'clock and stayed offshore fishing until nearly dusk. He had been drowned in the big wind of 1926.

Dad died Friday. Mum taken to hospital with heart attack. Please come soon.

We drove through a construction site, pale with yellow dust and noisy with trucks, cranes, and shovels. Through a rift in the dust I caught a glimpse of a barren landscape, rolling, tundralike country, a river, blue hills set against black clouds. It was blotted out as the car tipped into a river bed and bounded over water-washed rocks.

The hitchhiker's uncle had left the outport and had become the skipper of a banker, a fishing schooner that worked on the Grand Banks, the great fishing territories southeast of Newfoundland. He had returned to the outport when the hitchhiker's mother died and had taken the seventeen-year-old boy away with him. He felt the boy should have some schooling; it was ridiculous for such a bright youngster to be unable to read. But no school would take him. The banker captain had taught the boy to pick out words and to add. Since that time, he had read hundreds of books, but "I don't write so well."

We climbed a curved and dusty incline which led into mountains, the caps of which were obscured in mist. Suddenly, it was dark, although it was still morning.

The lights of other cars moved in the misted hills. The hitchhiker saw nothing, intent on examining his memory.

His uncle had died in 1937, leaving the eighteen-year-old boy to take care of himself. It was depression time. The youngster walked, sometimes on roads, sometimes across the barrens. He caught a rabbit and slept where some caribou had camped. He came to a coastal village and a storekeeper gave him fifty cents worth of food on credit. If the youngster could catch a couple of barrels of Christmas fish, he wouldn't owe the storekeeper a thing. Christmas fish? What were they?

He learned they were small fish that could be caught through the ice. He stole a net, borrowed an ax, and went fishing. He got the two barrels, all right, and lived on fish and slept in an old shed. In fact, he caught a dozen barrels of fish, and with the credit, bought shotgun shells. The storekeeper lent him an old gun and he hunted ducks all winter. He sold them to the storekeeper for ten cents each. He enjoyed that winter, he did, and was sorry when the ducks disappeared to breed in the north.

John due at Joe Batt's Arm Tuesday. Please arrange to meet the boat.

He got through the summer. But in the fall he took sick. It was the TB. Everybody had it then. Something to do with a lack of green vegetables, people said. He spent the next two years in and out of hospitals, and then got into the war. The army doctors never found out about his TB. But the English officers were a problem. Perhaps he was biased against them. It was difficult, though, to talk about the British. The British had always run Newfoundland. It was their first colony and they regarded it as their own. They took the codfish out of the sea and carried them home. But they put nothing back into Newfoundland, and this left the island in poverty, at the fringe of the greatest fish bounty on earth. Yet, somehow, they made Newfoundland glad to be British.

The darkness lightened suddenly and it began to rain, torrential, tropical-style rain. In seconds it filled the craters in the road. Cascades of water rose from under the wheels of passing cars. The car crawled with mud. Water hit like a wet towel whacking a concrete floor. The wipers could barely deal with the muck and the grille under the windshield clogged with what looked like the spoilings of a sluice dredge.

The hitchhiker's father had run his life on credit, perforce, because he rarely saw money in cash form. He ran up a bill at the village store for his fishing provisions, and it was a funny thing, you know, that it did not matter how many fish he caught, he could never pay off the bill. He never really knew how much he got paid for his fish. He trusted the storekeeper, who was a man of education, a man who could *read* and *write*!

Bill and Mary arriving from Boston on the car ferry Thursday. Expect to see you all at the reunion.

When the store bill got out of hand, the storekeeper asked his father to build him a dory, or maybe two dories, if it was a big bill. Dory-building was hard work in a land where the forests had been exploited for lumber and firewood for hundreds of years. Forests grew slowly on the island. His father spent his winters building dories, and counting the time he spent traveling to the nearest woodland and bringing out his lumber, he worked for a little more than five cents an hour. The store was owned by a merchant in St. John's, and *he* sold the dories, presumably for a nice profit.

The hitchhiker's uncle had lived according to the same rules, though by island standards he was a successful man. He worked for merchants who owned the schooner he skippered. In those days, the fishing business was always in hard times, at least, so his uncle claimed. Markets were bad. He was lucky to be a skipper for those people. They would always take care of him, they would. And they did. After fifty years at sea, he was pensioned at seventy-five dollars a month. In his best year at sea, he made twelve hundred dollars and his men made two hundred and fifteen each. That was for more than four months at sea. It had to last them for the year, though, because there was no other work. The owners traveled a lot, in Europe mostly, and the uncle sometimes got letters from them with pretty stamps on the envelopes. Their children went to school in England. Of course, you had to understand that everything in England was much better than here. Newfoundlanders were a poor people and they had to be thankful that England had always tried to take care of them.

Ahead, the road turned black, smooth, straight. With relief, I drove the car onto blacktop again. But to my astonishment, I found the surface had emulsified to a depth of half an inch. I was driving over molasses spread between the shoulders of the Driveway. It was so thick that it lifted from the wheels reluctantly, like a wet wool blanket pushed by wind. I slowed, thinking I would wait until the rain stopped; but a truck passed me and buried the car under a solid wave of the muck. The windows were blacked out. The wipers crawled across the windshield, half cleared it, but another car passed and I was blacked out again.

I passed two cars whose drivers had decided to stop. The cars were rounded, shiny-black cocoons. Higher speed helped, I found. The harder the black stuff was struck, the more it tended to disintegrate. But at higher speed, even a second's loss of visibility was dangerous. I changed my driving technique. I approached a black wave fast, smashed into it, wound down the window, and drove with my head out the window until the wipers cleared the windshield. I risked meeting another car, of course, in the window-down phase, with consequences too horrible to think about.

At last, the melted blacktop ended and the car slewed into deep sand. The sand and the liquid asphalt created a magnetic union. Within a mile, the car was caked in sandpaper.

Dave leaves for Toronto in a few days. Can we all get together?

How had the hitchhiker managed since the war?

Well, it had been a bit of this, and a bit of that. A man could sometimes get work in a fish plant or in the lumber camps. For the last three months, he had been helping build the Driveway, working for a mainland contractor.

What doing?

He was driving a bulldozer, and there was a bit of a story to *that*. The road builders were desperate for skilled men because few mainlanders wanted to work on the island. So he had hidden in the bushes and watched the men at work. After a few days, he had memorized the things the bulldozer drivers did, the levers they pulled, and so forth. He had applied for a job, and the foreman had said, "All right, let's see you drive this one," and, no doubt about it, he had been some scared then. But he had got up and yanked those levers and away he went with a rush. He had been getting good money ever since. Now, if I would slow down a bit here, he would get out.

We were on a lonely stretch of road, with only a rough, tar-paper shack visible against a hill.

Here?

"Yes," he said. "I'm going fishing for a few days, and that's my shack. Much obliged for the lift, and good-by, sir." He nodded.

In that last word was almost all I ever needed to

know about these island people. He walked through some alders and disappeared.

The schooner is bringing Dad down from the Labrador this week. We are making all the arrangements at this end. He will be laid to rest on Friday.

Today, the Devil's Driveway has gone. The dust, the potholes, the insane stretches of mud and sand, the washouts and the liquid asphalt have disappeared. You drive through a blur of beech and spruce on a road almost indecently civilized in such primeval territory. You may stop, get out, and listen. The silence is perfect at first; then you hear the faint music of songbirds. A flock of redpolls twinkles overhead and a hidden stream mutters among a glistening line of aspens. Hills sweep down to earth. A solitary raven circles.

I remember the old Driveway. To me it was a symbol of the island's four hundred years of history, a history that Newfoundlanders had accepted as being the way of the world.

At the height of its disheveled life, it personified an island people entering the twentieth century. They were late, exploited, poor, but they very definitely were arriving. Determined to escape from the old days of their isolation, they wanted to be like the rest of us. In the same way as the running eiders, they had to abandon the island, or at least, the traditional idea of it. They had to find out what the world was all about.

4

The Edge of the Labrador

UNK ISLAND pulls the traveler toward it, and once under its influence, it is impossible to turn back. It lies within reach of the arctic, midway between the Grand Banks and the coast of Labrador and so is not near anything or, today, on the way to anywhere. In the old days, many schooners sailing for the north foundered on the rocks that barely break the surface around the island. Today, no Labrador-bound ship will go near Funk Island.

It is impossible to fly to the island. For most of the year, weather makes a landing from a boat not feasible. The coincidence of calm seas, light winds, and a willing boatman occurs so infrequently that few outsiders, or Newfoundlanders, have ever managed to reach the island.

But the legend of Funk Island is well diffused. As the traveler moves along the Driveway from Port aux Basques, heading for Valleyfield, which is the best jump-off port for Funk Island, he passes through more than five hundred miles of indoctrination for his destination. The people along the road have heard of Funk Island, and they talk about it. They know it is significant. What for? They are not sure.

But at the turnoff, where the road to Valleyfield cuts away from the Driveway and turns northward along the east coast, the myth of the island becomes more influential. The people here have been accustomed to having a road for only a few years and they are closer to more superstitious times. They look toward Funk Island with ancestral respect.

"A hard, hard place, sir."

The villages look out at the Atlantic, hamlets held in a breath of stillness. Mainlanders who see them for the first time can mistake their aspect for death. The houses sit lightly on the land, as though their occupants have no faith in living there. The coast is utterly bare, the forest long since cut back by relentless axes, or driven from the shore by winter winds that can draw the air out of your lungs.

I drove into Valleyfield between houses perched on rocky shores. The road wound under the windowsills of old stores and leaning churches and a hundred blind windows glinted in a falling red sun. I was a long way from home here, and the people leaned on shovels and out of windows and watched the foreign car, silently intent on its details and driver.

Funk Island is present at Valleyfield. When I asked a stranger for directions, he leaned in my car window and said: "You be the feller a'goin' to the Funks?" Newfoundlanders pluralize the island's name, probably because there are actually two islands there, the second one a scrap of rock adjoining the main island. I was puzzled until I remembered I had made an arrangement

to charter a fishing boat to take me to the island. I pulled
into a gas station to get a gashed fuel tank repaired and
a broken windshield replaced. A woman attendant said,
with finality: "You're the man what's goin' to the Funks,
that you are." At a fish-processing plant, the manager,
Marvin Barnes, was envious. "I've never been there. It
must be quite a sight. They say there's a million birds."

Funk Island changed its character in this atmosphere and acquired a distinct underlay of the sinister.
How could any island influence so many people with its
empty presence? *A'goin' to the Funks* took on a deeper
meaning with each hour I spent in Valleyfield. The
people treated me as an explorer. I was going to the far-
off places and they recognized that they could not follow
me. The island was for mad outlanders. More than four
hundred years before me, Jacques Cartier had landed
there and was dumbfounded. ". . . our two boats went
thither [to the island of birds, as he called it] to take
in some birds whereof there is such a plenty that unless
a man did see them he would think it an incredible
thing. . . ."

After Cartier came fishermen, whalers, and sealers
to whom the island was a repository of fresh meat and
eggs. They used it relentlessly until, by the end of the
eighteenth century, the great auk had been wiped out
and the other sea birds on the island were depleted. All
that remained, in legend form, was the word *penguin*,
the original name of the great auk. This was soon lost
officially to another breed of flightless creatures, in the

Southern Hemisphere. But in Newfoundland, the word is immortal, changed to suit the dialect. The *pemwems* are now mythological.

I ate supper alone in a tiny restaurant, one bare room with a rickety chair and a jukebox of old records. The bright eyes of two waitresses gleamed through a chink in a burlap curtain, and I heard a fierce whisper:

" 'e a'goin' to the Funks."

I sat on the wharf at Valleyfield and waited. The sun was brilliant and small in the west; its rays glided over the caps of waves ridging the harbor. Half a dozen Cornish-eyed children watched me covertly. This was a long spasm of time. The place was peaceful. A two-story frame house, floating on old oil drums and towed by a fishing boat, passed by. The kitchen flue smoked and I could see the housewife through a window, preparing supper.

New York lay at an illimitable distance. The thrusting buildings, the sleek crowds pushing down into Grand Central, the anxious, closed faces of Negroes and Puerto Ricans, the hissing cabs and shuttling lights, seemed so far away that I had to wonder whether this, or that, was the world of Homo sapiens.

My traveling had given me the gift of isolation. I was free. Nothing demanded my attention. There was no need for action, thought, or courtesy; for kindness, rage, or recrimination. I could lie on the wharf and sleep, or get drunk, or jump into the water, or run a mile, or if I felt like it, make the harbor disappear with a flick of my eye. I was in a Hegelian state of release; what I had seen and done was acting inside me in a compression of youthful energy.

As I floated in thought, the *Doris and Lydia*'s diesels growled in the distance. She was a longliner, a vessel which spun out a filament of thread more than a mile long into the water, studded with thousands of hooks. She had been prowling the banks, the plateau pastures of the ocean, in search of codfish herds. She slid into the wharf, and her crew grinned a diffident welcome to their customer, the stranger from New York. The ship was moored, the engines died, and the men came ashore.

They were archetypes, unchanged in appearance or custom over three hundred years of Newfoundland history. They were *sea*-men, so constantly exposed to the ocean that they were formed by it. Brown faces wrinkled from squinting into sun and mist, hands ripped by hooks, burning ropes, and dogfish teeth, and the beginning of a gnarling and twisting process in their limbs that is the product of the elemental life. Their bodies concealed a kind of dynamic strength that came from a will to do and an acceptance.

Captain Jacob Sturge came ashore first, a big, bearish man, grinning widely. He shouted something incomprehensible and rocked along the wharf to secure a warp. Arthur Sturge, his eldest son and the real captain of the ship, followed. He was lean, grinning too, with the authority of a master. He was followed by Jacob's other sons, the crewmen and partners in the longline venture:

reflective Perce, shy Avalon, Willie, withdrawn and also shy, young Cyril.

Jacob Sturge came back along the wharf, still bellowing. Then Arthur Sturge began talking, and I could not understand either of them. The other boys made noises in the background. Not that it mattered; I understood nothing. Newfoundland is a dialect hunter's dream. The accents range from sing-song inflections of educated community leaders in the cities through infinitely various gradations of English spiced with touches of Irish, Welsh, and Scottish.

However, to suggest the speech of these men does them a disservice. To write their language (and even phonetics are inadequate to record the sound of it) caricatures them. It diminishes their dignity and character. But *not* to hint at their accents and method of speech is to ignore what makes them, outwardly at least, absolutely unique. How to write this roaring, this mangling of vowels, sentences, even ideas? All I can do is delineate phraseology and accents, and perhaps the imagination will supply the growling voices, the sudden bursts of passion and anger, the rough glitter of ideas buried in speech that is really archaic.

"Eee raaag aaaaht tamaarrr, arrrr!" Jacob bellowed.

For a moment, I thought he was joking and looked at him, uncomprehending. "Eeeeaaaaeghngahn na dar," he bellowed on happily, thinking that by simplifying the thought, he would get me to understand him. "Oh, ahhrrr," he said. "Eeeagoahnaredempemwemswar!"

Suddenly, I got part of the message. Pemwems! Then I had the last word of the sentence: "war" meant "were," so the sentence ended with the phrase "where the penguins were." Before I could finish my analysis of Uncle Jacob's sentence, his sons began to talk. Arthur Sturge's voice was not a happy bellow like his father's. It was a powerful nasal growl, like the meshing of gears in a big truck.

"Eeegoahngtde *Funks*!" he said from behind a limp, homemade cigarette. Finally, like an Egyptologist with his Rosetta stone, I had a key to the structure of the language.

" 'E goahng t' de Funks." "You [ye] going to the Funks."

Then Avalon was speaking and words were emerging. "Dem Funks," he said, "dey is a hard place."

Willie spoke. "Y'never been der?"

I said no.

"Do 'e know dey's arnted?" Perce asked the others, and they all laughed. I was not surprised. Of course the Funks would be haunted.

As I made my first efforts to join the conversation, I found that communication between these men was based on mutual knowledge which, in their circumscribed world, clearly was more important than mine. For instance, one of the men said: " 'E garn darn thar?" He was asking whether a mutual friend was going up to the Labrador coast to work that summer. The answer was "Yar." Both men understood what their friend was doing; how much money he was making; how long he would stay away; when and how he would come back.

Much of the time, I could only catch the sense of what the men were saying and had to fill in the difficult passages with imagination. The talk was bare communication, stripped to essentials. Unimportant phrases were reduced to an unintelligible growl, or left out altogether. Uncle Jacob gestured toward the sunset, which had become spectacular. He shouted suddenly: "Rrrrrrrrrrrrrrrrr—k—at?"

I got that, all right—verbal shorthand. "At," obviously, was "that." The sentence was a question, the "k" was the ruined remains of "like," and the growl preceding it would have to be "How do you . . ."

This was easy enough. But the construction of some sentences was so baffling I had no clue except instinct or imagination. "E be goo' far arrr?" meant "Would that be a good thing for us [or "for you"]?" One man, in a classic combination of verbal abbreviation and archaic construction, shouted suddenly: " 'E thar?" He was asking whether a compatriot had gone to live in the United States. The United States is always "thar." The word is affectionate.

As my understanding of the language grew, I partially entered their world. Their shyness diminished and they talked about "the old times," and particularly "the hard times," both of which had enduring significance. Their conversation shaped a force among us as we roamed amid the codfish with our talk and winched in the longlines, with their thousands of passive fish. The force, presence, whatever it was, grew pungent: the smell and the sound of the sea.

The reminiscences went on while the Valleyfield harbor behind the men turned purple as the last light of the day withdrew over low hills. A solitary tern flew past and disappeared out to sea. One of the men, a homemade cigarette dangling from his lip, spat into the water. He seemed about to speak but then settled down with a shudder of his shoulders.

I knew his feeling. When I was a youngster, on the night before the wheat harvesting began, I would shiver with excitement at the thought of the snapping exhausts and spinning pulleys drawing a twelve-foot sea of wheat into the combine. This fisherman, who would never see a wheatfield, felt the same unalloyed anticipation. He would tell tales about it in the future. A strange man, a tall man, came from New York, he did, and he wanted to go to the Funks; a strange fellow.

The talk swung around to the Funks. It was their most distant fishing ground, the most difficult and dangerous place to fish. But when the fish came in there, it was the best fishing of all.

" 'E remember the big blaw, now when war it?" Uncle Jacob shouted. "Y'know, when Poor Cap'n John, 'e went down."

"Nar," Arthur Sturge said, "y'mean Poor Cap'n Peter."

"Oh aar!" Uncle Jacob shouted. "Poor Cap'n Peter, that be right!" He turned to me.

"Poor Cap'n Peter, 'e war out to de Funks," he went on, "an' up came dis big blaw, came all of a sudden, no warnin' at all, at all."

Arthur Sturge took up the story. "Some of dem," he said, "dat war out at de Funks, dey wore away well out to sea and *dey* got back because dey had *room* to move."

Uncle Jacob spoke again. "But poor John . . ."

"Cap'n *Peter*," Arthur Sturge said.

"Poor Cap'n Peter," Uncle Jacob corrected himself. " 'E came straight down de coast, and y'know, 'e 'ad all his boys wid 'im. Dey was out to de Funks for de first time, an' only because dis war his last trip for de season."

Arthur Sturge: "Dey said he had a rotten rudder."

Uncle Jacob: "Aahhhr, aahhhrr! 'E come straight down dat shore, 'e did, in de black of night."

Arthur Sturge: " 'E come up against one of dem islands."

Uncle Jacob: "Ahhhr, dat 'e did, dat 'e did."

Poor Cap'n Peter was one of many who had died fighting their way back home rather than spend a night safely offshore.

"Oh-aaahhhhhrrr!" Uncle Jacob said, "dat Funks are a 'ard place, all right!"

It scarcely matters that these men go to sea with diesels under them instead of a thousand square feet of canvas. They are, essentially, the same people as poor Cap'n Peter. However, today they believe they have a right to survive. Cap'n Peter would have been fatalistic about his chances.

Theirs had been a fatalism based on ignorance; they talked about education with deep envy. In Uncle Jacob's generation, a man went to school when he was not fishing. His boys had done a little better, but not much. Arthur Sturge described it:

"It war loike a smarl sip of water when yar dyin' of thirst."

They talked on and revealed a self-contained world without smugness or prejudice, fear or distrust. They were pure men, straight men, if you like, and if men like this were the product of ignorance, I could make a good argument for the abolition of education.

"Now," Uncle Jacob said to me, "ye been in a smarl boat before?"

I said I had.

" 'E strong down here?" he asked, slamming a big fist against his broad stomach.

"Oi don' t'ink 'e knows about de longliner," Willie said, grinning.

"She goes up," Avalon said, inclining his hand vertically, "an' den she comes down." He declined his hand sharply, and all of them laughed.

" 'E can laugh," Perce said, referring to me, "but can 'e sail?"

"Nar," Willie said. "Oi t'ink de longliner will be too strong for 'im."

They were discussing a simple and benevolent measure of a man. Would I vomit? If I fell into the scuppers, well and good. If I did not, they would know something about me. They understood primal qualities: endurance, stoicism. How would I behave?

"Oh dem pemwems," Uncle Jacob said. "Dey must have been a soight to see. Dey was on de Funks, sir, so thick dat dey did cover her!"

Almost every man, conscious of the natural world or not, feels the tug of creatures, or men, made extinct: Hadrian's footsteps in the Forum, Chopin's dead piano, the silence of Stonehenge, the son of a man who fought at Waterloo. I had felt this in imagined or real communication with the past.

In the same manner, Funk Island is a monument to the past. You listen for the sound of the great auk. It is so close, *almost* within living memory, yet so distant that we know nothing of its voice (a bark? a scream?) and little of its habits. Funk Island is its Forum.

I asked if Uncle Jacob's father, grandfather, or great-grandfather had had any stories about the pemwems. He was vague. "Oh yar," he said doubtfully. "My fader, yar, my fader, he talked about 'em."

But when I quizzed him about his grandfather and great-grandfather, he became more doubtful. "Oh dey *seen* 'em, all right."

Yes, but had they told stories about them?

"Well," Uncle Jacob said, scratching his head, "dem pemwems war *everywhere!* Dey war just out dar." He gestured to the open sea. "Dey was on all de oislands!"

But how did he know this? Who had told him? He was vague again.

"My fader, 'e told me."

But who had told his father?

"My grandfader, 'e tell of dat."

So he must have seen them?

"Oh, 'e seen 'em, all right."

But had his grandfather told stories about them? Where did they go in winter? How many were there? Vague again, but "Yar, yar, 'e tell, all right, but dem stories is lost now."

The trail back to the great auk was too long. Odd auks were reported in the western Atlantic until around 1830. Uncle Jacob's grandfather probably could not have seen one. The great-grandfather might have, but Uncle Jacob's fumbling among his memories produced nothing but a chaos of impressions.

Arthur Sturge cut into the conversation. "Now thar be one man who *really* knows about dem Funks. Old Uncle Christopher, he really knows dem Funks."

"More dan Uncle Benny?" Avalon asked.

"Yar," Arthur said. "Much more dan Uncle Benny. He knows more dan anybody."

"Yar roight!" Uncle Jacob shouted, as the memory struck him. "Now oi remembers! Uncle Christopher, 'e knows about dem Funks, that 'e do! Whoi, 'e war a man who really seen dem pemwems!"

"He seen them?" I said incredulously.

"Oh yar, 'e done that!" Uncle Jacob said confidently.

"When?"

"Well . . ." He scratched his head. Then he shouted at Arthur. "Uncle Christopher, how old 'e be now?"

I jumped to my feet. "He's still alive?"

The Sturges ignored me. Arthur rolled a new cigarette. "Well now, let me see, Uncle Christopher, 'e now be about one hundred and ten."

Uncle Jacob snorted. "Nar, nar, more loike 'e be one hundred and twenty or more."

According to Jacob's reckoning, this fabulous old man would have been ten in 1854. If he had seen a great auk, it would be the last authentic sighting of an auk anywhere, like meeting a man who had fought at Waterloo. But as the Sturges wrangled on about Uncle Christopher's age, I realized they were using an old Newfoundland custom of continuing to count the years of a man's life after he was dead. Uncle Christopher was long since in the ground, and now, of course, I had to doubt Jacob's recollections of him. Had he really seen the pemwems?

"Nar, nar," Arthur Sturge said, " 'e never seen dem pemwems."

Jacob exploded. " 'E *talked* about dem!"

Arthur was patient. "Yar, but we *all* do dat."

The men were silent for a moment, as puzzled as I by the elusive auk.

I looked at them and it was my conceit, for a second, that I knew their thoughts. Perce's long, somber face was turned toward the dead water which lay between

us and the sunken sun. He was more thoughtful than
the others, possibly because he had recently recovered
from a dangerous operation which had saved his life. "I
crossed into the other world, but I came *back!*"

Arthur looked out to sea where, if he were skillful
and lucky, he would drive the *Doris and Lydia* among
enough codfish to keep six families in food and funds
for another year.

Avalon and Willie quietly rolled new cigarettes.
They would crew the boat and accept their chances.
Cyril hunched, perhaps thinking of himself and the day
when he would leave the crew and find his fortune away
from the damned sea.

"Oh yar," Uncle Jacob said. "But there's Uncle
Benny. 'E's alive! Uncle Benny knows about dem Funks.
Uncle Benny's the man to see. Uncle Benny's your man!"

5

Old Uncle Benny

THE WEATHER CLOSED IN around Valleyfield. I heard the sea roaring beyond the calm of the harbor. The Funks receded and left me empty in my mind. I wanted to be aboard the longliner and heading north, regardless of the weather. But no boats moved anywhere in the harbor. I could see the *Doris and Lydia*'s masts standing behind a cluster of frame houses. When I met Uncle Jacob rolling along a narrow dirt track, I knew what I wanted, and he expressed it for me.

"Let's go and see old Benny."

Long before I talked to the Sturge boys I had known about Uncle Benny, though not by name. Years ago, a Newfoundland friend had told me: "There's an old fellow up on the east coast somewhere who sails without even a compass. He goes off to some godforsaken island in thick fogs and storms. They say he'd put to sea in a paper bag. His sense of direction is supposed to be uncanny."

This had made little impression on me at the time. Newfoundland is full of such stories. But when I talked to the Sturges, I realized the old man sailing to sea in a paper bag was no legend; he existed, and I must meet him. Arthur Sturge had paid him a mariner's compliment: "Dat man," he said, "has got latitude."

Benjamin Sturge lived in a frame house overlooking a small cove. The land around him was rugged rock, sparsely touched with grass. From his house he could see the island where he was born in 1887. He could see another island too, an island where most of his children died. He could look down a slope under his bedroom window to where his schooner was moored.

Uncle Benny was an islomaniac. Even in winter he could not keep away from islands. He marooned himself on lonely offshore scraps of land and spent weeks hunting ducks. For more than sixty years he had fished at the Funk Islands among pinnacled, half-submerged rocks, eccentric currents and squalls, in waters that most fishermen shunned. There was a mystic union between him and the Funks and, indeed, any island. "An island is like a good woman; it's just there when you need it," a fisherman had told me once. This was Uncle Benny's credo too.

As we neared Benny's house, Uncle Jacob shouted a greeting from the open car window. An answering foghorn boom came from the house.

I watched the two old men slapping each other's backs and bellowing at one another—they had not met for several days—and I was astonished that conversation could be carried on at such a level. When Uncle Benny turned on me, I drew back. He *communicated*. His message was important. He *would* be heard. He was almost toothless in the mid-upper jaw, and he liked to talk at close range—about six inches. I was deafened. Uncle Jacob beamed in the background.

At first, I understood nothing. All my attention was occupied by his two black teeth, the working tongue, the bobbing uvula, the sea-wrinkled cheeks, the small eager eyes. Air blasted up out of his lungs, roared through his voice box, and sometimes laden with spittle, hurtled toward me. His accent, or dialect, or whatever it might be called, was much coarser than that of the Sturge boys. Was this English? I knew many regional English accents but nothing like this. Many Newfoundlanders, I discovered later, could not understand him.

His two sons, Harold and Henry, were in their forties. They gathered at our elbows, gap-toothed and grinning, delighted for a chance to shout at the stranger. Both had voices like ripsaws tearing into hardwood. Harold roared out a phrase, Henry embellished it, and Uncle Benny broke in with the punch line. They all shouted, laughter gushing out of those incredible, castellated mouths. Uncle Benny bellowed a question at me; Harold rephrased it; Henry repeated it; Uncle Jacob translated it; I responded. The men whooped with laughter. "Oh arrrrrr, oh arrrrrr!" they shouted, tears streaming down their cheeks.

If I did not understand everything Uncle Benny said, I certainly knew I was close to a fountainhead of energy and passion, a powerhouse. It was not possible to equate this man with anyone I had ever known. How can I recreate his spirit? There are no modern terms of comparison. He was so crude, so basic, that he achieved a gentle, haunting pathos, a preservation of older ages and values. His forebears came from England in the 1700's. They were illiterate fishermen. *Their* forebears may have fought the Armada. Isolated in Newfoundland, they preserved the maritime vigor of the old country and the classic, bittersweet flavor of life suggested in the music and literature of the sixteenth and seventeenth centuries.

> All our joys,
> Are but toys,
> Idle thoughts deceiving.
> None have the power,
> Of an hour,
> In themselves bereaving.

As Benny roared on, I felt this gay-sad emanation and clearly heard music. Orlando Gibbons' magnificent variations on "Wood So Wilde" ran like a sinew through my imagination. I could see Benny in the music—exuberant, reckless, touched with sadness but affirmative to the death. Like the ancient ethic that preceded him, Benny existed for something. He might not play the lute or plunder the Main but it was clear he lived for a purpose, and that purpose was represented by the brooding presence of Funk Island.

The island wove in and out of his stories like a ghost. It obsessed his thoughts. It was where "the black winds blow," and "the best place to be in all the world." The island drew him, manipulated him, made him fearful and respectful. He loved it with a lasting passion.

My representation of his speech is only a simplified translation from the original. But listen to him.

"Thar war many hard toimes at de Funks, roight dar war. But let me tell ye somethin' fair, now. Oi can always git to de Funks, day or noight, oi can, in starm or fog, it doan't matter, oi can always git thar.

"Now let me tell ye about dem Funks! Dat are a place to keep away from, rocks an' toides loike ye moight dream of, oh yar! So whoi do oi fish at dem Funks? Because dat whar de cod are, sir! My grandfarder, 'e did fish der, 'e did, and 'is farder before 'im, an' 'is farder before 'im. Moi great-grandfarder, 'e did tell stories of dem pemwems on dem Funks, oh yar, dat 'e did, but dem stories be arl larst now, sir, arl larst!"

Gradually, the archaic phrasing and mangled words began to make sense and formed speech that had a strange, raw beauty.

"Now let me tell you about them Funks! At night when them winds is blowin', the island do make a kind of howlin' noise, and it do make you think a bit, I can tell you that, sir! One night, I got caught there in a bad blow, a very heavy wind. I got in behind that island but the engine it would not haul me by itself so I put up the sail and I kept tackin' back and forth and when I got out of the lea of the island, I would turn right sharply, and that way, I kept she in the lea of the island. Sometime after the dawn, the wind it did let up and I were able to anchor. Oh, that were a time, sir, that it were!"

He found this hilarious. His hand smashed down on my knee with a report like a pistol shot, and he erupted with laughter. "Oh, oh," he shouted, "that were a time, sir!" He looked at me for a moment, the laughter dying, his eyes quizzical and I knew a judgment had been made about me.

"Now let me tell you about them turrs." ("Turr," I knew, was the Newfoundland word for "murre.") "Now boy, them birds, they do know a thing or two. Before them gannets come to the island, them turrs just never would get together to go to sea with the young ones. But then the gannets come to the island and they would catch many of them young turrs, oh, yes, I seen that! Swallow them right down! So them turrs, they got together and they formed up these long lines, like they was in a big army and they marched to the sea and that's the way them turrs, they did beat them gannets."

I did not disabuse Uncle Benny. The murres always go to sea in masses, but his story was too charming, too much original folk art in action for me to question.

He bellowed on through his labyrinthine memory of Funk Island; how a dozen big bankers, schooner-rigged fishing vessels, would anchor at the island at the turn of the century, and their crews would go ashore to plunder the birds and eggs. They rigged up big chutes from island to dory and slid hundreds of barrels filled with eggs down them.

The banker crews amused themselves, when their work was done, by running through the massed thousands of murres until "there were a'scattering and a'screaming, sir, like you would never forget!" He recalled whaling days at the island when he would anchor on a nearby shoal and jump off his schooner onto the backs of dead whales moored there by whalers who had gone off on another hunting expedition.

At night, he would hear the rushing murmur of the island's multitude ("they never sleep") rising and falling in the wind and, in the distance, see the lights of bankers "goin' up to the Labra-*dor*!"

Since the 1890's, when he began fishing at the Funks, he had seen the codfish diminish in size from giants of eighty pounds to fish of ten or a dozen pounds. "They are fishin' them out, sir, and them big ones, they are like the pemwems, sir, they are gone, gone."

Talking to Uncle Benny ultimately became exhausting. The proximity, the difficulty of understanding, the thunder of his voice, the need to concentrate, were enervating. He was dejected when Uncle Jacob said he must get home. We stepped out into bright sun, and Uncle Benny's voice carried across the cove to where his schooner lay at anchor, "Oh yar," he shouted, "I've seen some great times at the Funks and I can tell you a thousand stories."

As we walked down the track toward my car, I knew I could not possibly end our discussion this way, even though it had a note of finality about it. I asked him when he was going to quit fishing.

"In the fall, sir, in the fall, always in the fall, when the weather gets bad."

No, I said, I meant when was he going to leave the sea altogether.

At that, he broke into another spasm of laughter. "Oh, oh," he gasped. "Not never, sir, not never. I will never let that there boat go up on the mud, like all the others, no sir, I will not. As long as I can walk down this track to her, that's it. I'll stay fishing as long as I can walk to her, sir."

I asked him whether the schooner was the most important thing in his life. He was astounded.

"If you want to know, you must go to Flowers Island, where I was born to. Oh yes, sir." He shook his head. "It all be on Flowers Island. You can't understand till you've been to Flowers Island."

He looked at me and made his critical judgment. "I'll take you there," he said suddenly, "if you can be up at four in the morning."

In the car, driving with Uncle Jacob back to his village, we were quiet until Uncle Jacob said, "That man be an *island* man, and I know none like him."

The morning was cold and again with a bright, hard easterly blowing as we headed out to sea. In the boat with us were Uncle Benny's sons, Harold and Henry, and some friends to help him haul nets and traps. The two sons were known simply as 'Arold and 'Ig. Indeed, the apostrophes might just as well be dropped. There is no suggestion of an *H* in their names. Arold is demonstrably Arold. Ig, without question, is Ig.

As we headed into the wind, the land low, flat, green, at our elbows, icebergs rose in the distance, and terns jerked along beside the boat. Ig was at the tiller. As helmsman, he drove the boat along with a forward-and-backward motion of his body, like a bobsledder urging his vehicle down the ice. As he swayed, he crooned a little song to himself. The sound of it was lost behind the hammering of the single-cylinder engine amidships. Uncle Benny was in the bows, looking ahead to Flowers Island.

"It won't be long now," he shouted, rubbing his rough hands. "I can tell you, my boy, this be an island to see." He was in such a state of excitement that the other men grinned. Arold leaned forward and nudged me in the ribs. "Old man war born thar," he bellowed, indicating the island. In the stern, Ig grinned and nodded a delighted confirmation of this supremely important fact. He cupped his hands and shouted: "Old man war born thar!"

Flowers Island is undistinguished, a treeless lump of land unmarked by gully or gulch. Its rocky shore line contains one small beach. Its rounded green slopes are sheathed in subarctic grasses and berry-bearing plants which seem to spend months struggling out of the ground, never to reach the fruitional droop of high summer.

Yet this bleak scrap of land was Uncle Benny's spiritual home and once was the center of a thriving village. If Flowers Island has an epitaph, it is that man can live anywhere, and like Uncle Benny, draw lifelong inspiration from an abstraction. His belief in Flowers Island was a religious force. God was there, all right, in Benny's mind, and in moments of fervor he referred to the Great Master.

By eight thirty we had finished hauling a cod trap and four salmon nets and were heading into the island, while the men gutted the cod and salmon. The sun was brilliant, but it was bitterly cold on the water, about 39 degrees, although it was July 27.

There are actually two islands here, so close together they look like one. They are separated by a narrow channel which is called a *tickle* in Newfoundland. In the old days, this was a Venetian water street for the settlement.

We turned in toward the larger island, Flowers, with the smaller island, Sturge's, on our left. Uncle Benny leaped onto the gray rocks. Almost immediately he was on his knees, his hands scrabbling against the barnacled rocks.

"Look, look," he cried. "This were a dead man's hand." His fingers tore away some loose barnacles and exposed an inch-square piece of rusted metal buried in the rock. "Oh yar." He shook his head. "Them old folks knew how to make things last. Two hundreds years in there! I remember it, stickin' up, just like a dead man's hand—" he crooked his wrist so that his hand stuck up— "and you brought the boat in and tied it to this."

Then, suddenly, he was up and away across the rocks, his short bow legs pumping him along. As he moved, he shouted over his shoulder, "An' this where the store be," pointing to scrape marks, now barely distinguishable, on the smooth rocks. Then we were beyond the rocks and walking in thick grass. It would have taken an archaeologist to determine that once there had been a human settlement on this site. There was no sign of foundations, no discarded timbers, no stones anywhere.

Yet Benny was gripped by memory. The bitter chill of the arctic wind had given way to a tantalizing hint of warmth from the sun which overhung us. We climbed above the sea, flat and sparkling all around us. Beyond the sun a tall iceberg stood, still as stone. Uncle Benny reached a hollow among some longer grasses.

"An' this," he said triumphantly, "is where I were born!"

There are no ruins in Newfoundland because nothing is wasted. A house reaches the end of its life and is dismantled, timber by timber. Hinges, door handles, nails, bricks, pieces of mortar and cement, are re-used wherever possible. Twentieth-century boards are driven by eighteenth-century nails over nineteenth-century joists. Uncle Benny's home had, I knew, been long removed from the island and spread, in infinitely various form, along the nearby coast.

"An' that track," Benny said, pointing to a faint mark running uphill through the grasses, "is where my poor mother walked to her garden."

Disjointed, half-obscured in a running tide of reminiscence, the ancient life of Flowers Island grew around

me, close as a cloak. Here was the channel—no. Where
was it? Had it filled? Ah, here it was! No?—Well, anyway, the channel carried away the blood of the seals
when grandfather was dressing them. This was the root
cellar. ("My b'y, you could put a score of cabbages in
there in the fall, stick 'em in the ground, and they'd stay
fresh all winter.") To my eyes, the root cellar was two
stones, half-buried in a mound of earth. How could man's
occupancy be so completely obliterated?

As Uncle Benny talked, the village on Flowers Island
grew into a hundred houses, then shrank, as the same
names recurred, again and again. At last, surprisingly,
the village stood before me, a mere four houses, a couple
of stores, two slipways, half a dozen dead man's hands
driven into the rocks. Uncle Benny's world had been tiny
and intimate indeed. Yet its minuteness did not diminish
the vividness of his images.

There was nothing here to suggest the tenor of life
and its hardships except the memory of this old man. He
looked at the ground. "This war where we pitsawed," he
said doubtfully, as he sought a clue to the position of a
big hole he remembered.

Pitsawing was the most brutal physical work a man
could do. One man stood in a narrow pit holding the
bottom handle of a long ripsaw, while above him, standing on a platform, the second man gripped the other end
of the saw. Ripsawing—that is, cutting with the grain of
the wood—is hard work at any time, but when it is done
through green logs with one man hauling upward against

the combined weight of the saw and the bite of its teeth, while the bottom man is showered with sawdust, it becomes work for giants, at least by our standards. Once, when I was in hard physical condition, I lasted five minutes as the top man in an old pitsaw rig.

"My poor father," Benny said, "would saw here for fifteen to sixteen hours a day. I have seen him out here in the moonlight, *working alone,* as he tried to get all his work done."

We left the ghost village and the monotonous sough of the long saw, left long-dead children running from house to house, old Uncle Somebody dozing in the sun. ("They said he were more than a hundred.") Behind us were the phantom women endlessly digging gardens and turning long racks of drying fish as schooner crews clomped up the bare stone walks.

We mounted the backbone of the island, which led to the Lookout. As we walked, the Lilliputian history of the island grew around us. A small rock projected beside the path, and there, in the last century, two of the island's youngsters played with a cartridge, hitting it with a stone. It exploded and the bullet went into the head of one of the boys. In a ship under full sail, he was raced ashore with his family. The island's inhabitants mounted the Lookout to watch through a spyglass. An hour went by and the rescue ship headed for the island again. The man with the spyglass put it down. "Too late," he said. "Flag's at half mast."

The Lookout was, like the rest of the island, featureless. But on it we had a spectacular view of the sea around it. The thin line of the mainland ran along the western horizon and the eastern view was studded with icebergs of the Labrador Current.

Uncle Benny stood there in his childhood, and with a fascination for the Lookout that is still with him, watched the schooners. They passed endlessly on their way to the Labrador and the arctic, and young Benny may have seen the last of the big squareriggers heading to catch the last of the arctic whales. ("I seen some big ones, *four* masts!") He saw thousands of schooners: Newfoundlanders, Portuguese, French, Basque, Spanish, American, Canadian, British, as they beat north for the fabled coast of gold, the Labrador, swarming with its codfish bullion. From the time of his first memory until the schooners disappeared in the thirties, these ships changed little. They were two-masted, both masts carrying square sails gaff-rigged at the peak, the foremast holding two or three foresails with, perhaps, a pair of staysails between the two masts. The schooners were dark-hulled and the sails were brown, but when the wind was right, "they were like birds flyin'" as they swept past the island.

"Oh aye," Benny said, looking out over the empty, silent sea. "Them were the days."

The western slopes of Flowers Island were never settled, but every part of the island was used intensively during the two hundred years men lived on it. There was the make-believe ocean, a tiny pond of brown water, where Benny and other island youngsters had sailed toy ships all over the world. Beyond it, there was a cove with a solitary dory riding at anchor, perfect as an etching. There, the men had caught lobsters. Our feet crushed innumerable retiring flowers which would, in the fall, produce berries by the gallon. Benny and his sons once collected fifty-five gallons of cloudberries, which Newfoundlanders call bakeapples, and marshberries from this seemingly unproductive earth.

By now, none of the visible things were animating Benny's imagination. He was in another world, a winter world, as he stomped along the grass track. All his life, he had hunted the shores of Flowers Island for sea ducks, and he had killed between twenty and thirty thousand of them. The ducks had mystic significance for him, not only because they represented food and money, but because, throughout his life, in the hard times and in the good times, they had always come to Flowers Island.

The ducks are eiders. They breed in the lower arctic, and when winter begins they filter down the Labrador coast, seeking open water inshore where they can dive for shellfish on the sea bottom. Their numbers are prodigious, in the hundreds of thousands. The coast of Newfoundland bristles with duck-hunting guns but the eiders outbreed their losses. Benny had heard the ducks arriving since he was a child, usually during the first blizzard of the season, their presence signified by squawks and the swish of wings in the driving night skies.

Any ice around the island creates a hazard for the

gathering ducks. Without clear water, they cannot dive and will starve. They strive to keep patches of water open by settling in one area and smashing the forming ice with their wings and bodies. As the winter hardens, their numbers increase, and by February there are upward of fifty thousand of them feeding around Flowers Island.

Over the centuries, the island duck hunters have harvested this bounty from the sea and have even practiced conservation. Benny remembers that the head man of the island (always the dominant personality) did not permit duck hunting with a dog until after February 1. Then, it was "the good Lord for everyone and everyone for hisself."

The island's muzzle-loaders were taken out of dark corners, and while still caked with rust, the blood of old victims, the handmarks of long defunct hunters (they were never cleaned), they would be charged with black powder, wadding, and shot.

The lightest of these guns were American Civil War weapons, some with bayonets, a few of which are still in use today. They were dangerous, as evidenced by the occasional blind man and men with strangely powder-blackened faces. The heaviest of the old guns, far predating the Civil War, were closer to being artillery. Uncle Benny's heaviest gun, Big Bertha, was more than a hundred and fifty years old, and was loaded with a charge of powder and shot that packed the barrel for twelve inches. The recoil was unbelievable.

"Can't stand against *her*," Benny said.

The wise gunner made no attempt to withstand the impact, but let himself be hurled backward, the gun spinning over his head. Benny's best shot earned him forty-six ducks, though this was not a record in New-foundland. Arold was particularly fond of heavy charges and had a reputation up and down the coast as being "more dangerous to stand behind of than ahead of." Both Ig and Arold were enthusiastic gunners, light-fingered and daring on the trigger. Ig once fired at and brought down, a sea bird which landed on Arold's gun barrel. The gun, which was pointed at Ig, sputtered and went off. The charge narrowly missed Ig, but he was envel-oped in a sheet of flame. Arold extinguished the burning Ig before he was badly burned, but Ig was annoyed at his brother for laughing so much as he beat out the flames.

"It were a sight to see when we were firin' all together," Benny said, as we stood in the tiny cove over-looking the bright water.

Four men with these ancient guns had such muzzle power that Benny would enjoin each man to "watch the other man's barrel," to ensure a fair spread of shot. Then he would give the order to fire and the gunners would be sent spinning backward into snowbanks, their guns clattering overhead. The carnage among the ducks was dreadful, up to a hundred and fifty birds in a broadside.

The duck hunters were superbly casual about safety. Once, Benny and his boys were drying their powder in a shack on Flowers Island when a spark from the fire ignited the entire keg of powder. The explosion blew Ig through a wall, temporarily blinded Arold, and moved the building a foot off its foundations. The memory of this convulsed Benny. He pounded my shoulder. "Oh that were a funny time," he shouted. "I never seen the boys laugh so much in all my life!"

We had circumnavigated the island and were back at the tickle. Facing us was tiny Sturge's Island. I could see a small graveyard ringed by a picket fence.

"Now here," Uncle Benny shouted suddenly, "here was where the *Lady Kean* were launched."

Some time in the eighteen-eighties, a Flowers Islander named John Cole Kean decided to build a schooner. There was nothing logical about the idea. The nearest timber was nearly a score of miles away across the water. There were no shipyards on Flowers Island, indeed, no truly sheltered place to build a schooner at all. If Kean did build his schooner, he would have to launch it into the tickle, which is about as wide as the length of the average schooner. None of this stopped Kean. He and his island helpers chopped and sawed a hundred and odd tons of lumber, rowed it all out to the island and built a tall ship.

Benny and I crossed the tickle and climbed up the rocks of the smaller island. "And here," he said, "here, Sophie Kean stood and she had a bottle of rum in her hand. But nobody could think of a name for the schooner. She just stood on this rock and when the ship moved she threw the bottle and she did say, 'This ship will be named the *Lady Kean*,' and that, sir, was her name. And when she were afloat, one end of her stuck out over Flowers Island and one end stuck out over Sturge's Island."

He was moving inland through thick grass toward the graveyard, which even from the distance had an unreal look about it, like a single footprint in the sand. It lacked the confirmation of a nearby settlement. We passed a small mound where "the young feller had fallen." Half a century before, the islanders had used large cast-metal cauldrons for boiling down seal fat and extracting oil. A young fisherman had been tending a cauldron when the island's dinner bell was rung. In his haste to respond to the call for food, he had slipped and fallen into the boiling oil. No one could reach him in time and "you could hear them terrible cries on the island for years afterwards."

With the graveyard so close, it was easy to conjure up ghosts. Uncle Benny felt this more strongly than I. He stopped his headlong progress for a moment. "There were many hard times," he said. "Many terrible hard times." In theory, those island people never needed to starve. Any one of them could always catch enough fish for his family; his woman could always raise enough potatoes to last through the year. But the islanders were caught in an economic squeeze. To get their staples— flour, biscuit, beef, bacon, pork—they were tempted to sell as much of the fish they caught as possible. A man might put down three barrels of salted herring for the winter, but he might get such a poor price for his cod that he would sell a barrel of herring and hope for a short winter.

In 1893, the people of Flowers Island ran out of food by mid-February. The island was locked in ice which, at its periphery, had degenerated into slob ice, a tacky mixture of half-ice, half-sludge which was impassable for man or boat. With the food gone, with credit exhausted and cut off, the Flowers Islanders settled indoors to wait out the hunger.

"You could walk the island, my son, and not see another soul."

The very old and the very young ate the last scraps of food: half-rotten potatoes and bits of dried fish, improperly cured and gone green. Then, the worst blizzard of the year struck the island.

As he told the story, Uncle Benny stepped away from the mound of the cauldron. He faced inland and eastward, toward the low hump of the island's back which, like Flowers Island, was bare of anything except a thin layer of grass.

The morning after the blizzard, a shout reached the ears of the islanders on both sides of the frozen tickle.

"Water bear! Water bear!"

During much of the Newfoundland winter, ice pans flood into the Atlantic from the arctic. These pans bring down arctic foxes and occasionally polar bears. The bear who landed on Sturge's Island had probably drifted down from the coast of Labrador or Greenland, his hunting made difficult by the unpredictable opening and closing of the ice around him. He landed on the eastern side of the island. The main settlement was hidden from his view by a small hill. He climbed to the top of the island and looked down on the buildings lining each bank of the tickle, and he was spotted instantly.

Then it became a race. Skipper Sam Sturge was out of his house as the bear began its running retreat down the eastern slope. They had about the same distance to go. Skipper Sam reached the crest of the hill as the polar bear reached the tumbled ice pans at the shore. Skipper Sam fired, and the famine was over.

Uncle Benny was thoughtful, that single shot echoing across more than half a century. "The hard times," he said. "Oh them hard times."

The survival of the islanders often had nothing to do with the bounty of the sea or the beneficence of the seasons. "Poor Captain Billy Kean, he had a wonderful year. He shot three hundred ducks, and he killed three hundred seals, and he caught three hundred quintals of fish but, my son, the prices were so low he nearly starved the next winter."

As we walked toward the graveyard, I calculated that poor Captain Billy had hunted, by modern standards, nearly $14,000 worth of food, and I reflected that while jet planes and telephones gave me no sense of a changed or improved world, Captain Billy, starving in his sea of plenty, drove home the change surely enough.

We came to the graveyard. Some years previously, Uncle Benny and a friend had built a neat picket fence around it. They had tried to lift some of the fallen headstones, but there were so many they gave up. The cemetery was a junk yard of plants, broken stones, mounds, and glints of chipped marble in the grass. Here was the world of Uncle Benny's childhood, that nineteenth-century generation of islanders put into the soil before there was any thought of fleeing to the mainland.

They were unalloyed Anglo-Saxons: Sams and Johns, Marthas and Annes, Keans and Sturges. Uncle Benny had known many of them. Others, he knew by reputation. "Now, this man," he said, pointing to a stone, "he sailed to the seal fishery for twenty years and lost all his fingers, and he died with a cent in his pocket."

Another stone. "That man, he went into the foreign trade and never came back until he were very old. . . ." Oh, he knew these people, he did. But he was puzzled by something.

"You know, my son," he said, and his voice was quiet. "People don't care for them olden times any more. These stones could sink into the earth. Now, why are it a man from *New York* would ask about them people?"

For a second, it was my impulse to answer, to tell him about cities, and civilization, and the rest of the world. But the impulse died as I realized its futility.

We rummaged through the graveyard, lifting stones, speculating about the people under our feet, as though they still lived, or had but recently left us; this schooner builder, this duck hunter, that great cod trapper, or salmon catcher, this carpenter. Finally, in a corner of the graveyard, Uncle Benny slapped his hand on a tall white stone and said: "Now, this be the man that built the schooner, John Cole Kean, and his wife Sophie, and he be the man I remembers best, he be." I looked at the stone. It was not the name John Cole Kean, or Sophie Kean, inscribed on the white marble. Uncle Benny rattled on with his memorabilia, and I wondered what to do. I had supposed, long before this, that Uncle Benny was illiterate. Such deficiencies are overlooked by the wise mainlander. Yet I suspected he would prefer to know the truth.

"This isn't John and Sophie's grave," I said.

Uncle Benny seemed smaller for a moment. Our eyes met and we both knew what we knew.

"Who be down there?" he whispered.

Later, returning to the mainland, the sight of another island, a black chunk of rock surmounted by thin green grass, unleashed a further flood of shouted reminiscence.

This was Mickamackay Island. His family had settled here when the islanders left Flowers fifty-six years before to seek an easier life closer inshore or on the mainland.

Uncle Benny pointed to a channel twenty feet wide leading into a rocky cove. That was where he had sailed his schooner for safety in bad weather. He pointed to the crest of the hill, not more than a dozen feet above the level of the water. That was where the house had been; his home when the diphtheria came.

We have forgotten that diphtheria once was dreaded. It is hard to understand the terror it generated among those northern people. It struck Mickamackay Island in the late winter of 1924. For twenty-eight days and nights, Benny did not sleep. His oldest daughter, Claire, died, then his second daughter, Julia, and then his oldest son. The island was isolated because it was surrounded by impassable slob ice. The dead lay where they had died.

"Then," Uncle Benny said, "they came to the island with their caskets. But when I went to them, they walked away. They thought everybody had the disease. They were fearful.

"When the dead ones had gone, I got the diphtheria myself. I thought I were going at any moment, and I could not speak. I felt I was a'goin'. I made motions with my hands. They stood there and watched. They did not know what I meant. But my woman knew. She cut off a small piece of salt beef and I chewed it up and swallered it down. And, my dear man, it made a difference. In a moment, I hawked up the beef and what were chokin' me, and then I were all right, and I slumbered right off. But for a long, long time, it were hard to swaller. I would take a mouthful of tea and it would come spouting up out of me nose, and they would all laugh at me."

We were now in sight of his present house, perched up on its rock overlooking the shallow harbor.

"My wife's name were Karenhappuch," he said pensively. "That were after Job's daughter, in the Bible, my son. When I lost her twenty years ago, I lost my best friend, my right arm."

He remained thoughtful as we glided toward his ramshackle wharf. It had been a poor year so far for the cod fishery. But he would put the schooner in shape and go up to the Funks.

"I be in the fall of the leaf," he said (that magnificent Elizabethan phrase!) "but I feels just the same today as when I were twenty. I can still pull a heavy oar, oh yar!"

The previous winter, Ig had taken sick suddenly on Flowers Island when the men were hunting ducks. A helicopter was sent, in response to a signal fire, to bring him ashore, and word spread that Uncle Benny had died on the island. When the men arrived in the "elecop," a big crowd had gathered. As Benny got out of the aircraft, a man shouted: "We thart you were dead, Benny!"

Uncle Benny shook his fist and shouted: "Uncle Benny's not ready to go yet. I'll see most of you under the mud!"

It was late afternoon. We pitchforked the cod and salmon ashore, then walked up the short path to his frame house. The sun broke through rifted clouds, sending rays of smoky light across the water that lay between us and Flowers Island. We stopped and looked toward it.

"When I got back in the elecop," he said, "there were some who told me I were mad hunting the ducks when I were seventy-five. One man, he told me I could have died out there. I asked him what were wrong with that. I were *born* there!"

He was quiet for a long moment.

"If I had my wish," he said. "I would go back to the Flowers Island. Oh my dear son, I would end my days there."

6

The Funk Wind

THE DAYS OF WAITING stretched out interminably. The wind blew from the north; it blew from the east and then from the west. A deep swell formed from the south. Each day became a complex of useless calculations. Mist rolled in; if it cleared by midday, I could reach the Funks by evening. If the Sturges finished lifting the last of their nets by dusk, I could set out for the Funks immediately. If the wind blew from the land, it might dispel the overcast.

"We need a Funk wind," Arthur Sturge said.

On some days, with the Valleyfield harbor smooth, the wind light, a blue sky appearing intermittently in the overcast, I became convinced that the Sturges' reluctance to sail to the Funks was cowardice and obstinacy.

But one day there was a new smell in the air; I spent the whole day on the wharf, watching. By the time the *Doris and Lydia* growled into sight, it looked like a small cruiser. The trip to the Funks now had undertones of a voyage by Magellan, Cook, or Cartier. Uncle Jacob held a warp and grinned.

"Funks tomorrer, eh?" he yelled.

As the boat berthed, the wind veered to the south-

west (the Sturges had known it would) and became a
dry-land wind, a Funk wind. It would blow us up to the
island in the morning.

I was to meet the Sturges at three o'clock, which
meant getting up at two, which meant going to bed at
six in the evening. This seemed easy enough. Valleyfield
is sleepy at any hour.

But on this night, with the skies brilliantly clear
and the air warm, a group of neighborhood children
gathered on the lawn outside the staff quarters of the
fish processing plant and began a subhuman bedlam.
They must have been eviscerating each other. I could
hear small girls with limbs being torn from their sockets;
their screams were stilled by heavy blows. Little boys
pursued one another with razors and slashed off each
other's fingers. Their screams filled my room.

When they were not butchering each other, the children talked in pleonastic bellows. The cries went on
and on; the sky darkened; I twisted back and forth, and
my racing senses tingled. The prospect of the fabulous
Funks sent my imagination skittering. I remember midnight, the room oddly silent. I must have dozed some
time before one o'clock.

The sixty minutes of sleep passed in the blink of an
eye after seven wakeful hours. Nevertheless, there was
time for a brief nightmare.

I was on a large ship in heavy seas and near to the
Funk Islands. I strained to identify the island's birds
through the spume. A large, penguinlike bird shot skill-

fully out of the water onto a rock. It was, of course, a great auk, and I was at the island at an historic time. The world's last remaining great auk had been sighted.

A voice shouted: "There she goes!"

The island was sinking. Refugee birds scattered like planes from a stricken aircraft carrier. The great auk dived and disappeared. I awoke just as the alarm clicked, ready to ring at two o'clock.

The long-building excitement had charged me with such electric energy that I bounded out of bed as though I had enjoyed ten hours' sleep. It was impenetrably black outside, until I saw the stars. I dressed feverishly, checked clothes, cameras, film; eager hands trembled. Now that the moment was so near, I was caught by a combination of exhilaration at being on the move and the fear that something would go wrong at the last moment. My imagination flicked over the negative possibilities: mist, rain, too much swell, squalls.

The need to get all the equipment together and to leave the building without wakening anyone absorbed me. Soon, I was standing on the wharf, looking across black, silent water. Rexy Winters, the night watchman, stood with me. "My dear man," he said, with sudden concern, "are you going to the Funks with no boots?"

Yes, I was. Sneakers and light nylon clothing seemed more convenient.

"No, no," he said. "There's no knowing what might happen to a man up there. I'll get some boots."

Heavy sea boots not only keep a man's feet dry; they drown him quickly if he falls overboard.

In the distance one of the Sturges' diesels growled; then a second. The voyage to the Funks had begun.

A deep-sea trip on a longliner always has a touch of magic excitement about it, and the fishermen feel this, no matter how many trips they make. As we plunged into a swell toward the Labrador Current, we watched the roll of dusky waves lit faintly by the iridescent east. Cyril and Willie sat up forrard and were wet occasionally by spray kicked up from the short and violent pitching motion of the boat. Uncle Jacob stood at the wheel. Arthur, Avalon, and Perce smoked and looked ahead through the wheelhouse window, all immersed in that expectation which all men feel during the pre-dawn.

Sailing on a longliner is likely to be a rich sensory experience because of the gut-wrenching action of the boat, and its manifold smells. The long days spent at sea, the lack of washing facilities, the cramped quarters, and the need to be constantly at the ready, produce an atmosphere which, to put it mildly, is gamey. The *Doris and Lydia* was a clean ship, but some longliners I traveled on exuded incredible odors.

Any longliner is likely to smell of freshly spilled cod guts, of slime and fish scales, of blood and rubber boots, of pants and socks, of fried pork and wet timbers, of diesel fumes and oil, of coffee and frying haddock, of burned grease, wet gulls' feathers, and freshly eviscerated shearwaters.

We passed a dark island, a bare outline of hummocky rock and grass. Arthur Sturge gestured.

"That's Flowers Island. That's where Uncle Benny shoots ducks in the winter."

I visualized the island, surrounded by ice pans, and Uncle Benny stalking his duck prey. Arthur Sturge chuckled. "Once he were stuck there for three weeks during a blow, with his boy, Arold, and they were running out of food. One morning, Uncle Benny got up, and he said, 'Well, that be the end of the *eatables*; now, there's only *ourselfables!*'"

The eastern sky turned a rich, dusky saffron; the motion of the boat became increasingly violent. Sturge looked shrewdly at me.

"Do you feel all right?"

"Yes."

He nodded. "Most people who come with us are sick." He smiled at the memory. "There were one, a professor fellow, he were so sick he could not stand up. He lay there and he groaned and he were a sad sight to see. And then, we got to the Funks, and he *had* to get up. He said he'd come this far, he had to go on. We thought he would die. But we got him ashore. He were sick all the way back."

Sturge braced himself against a vicious lurch, which tore my hands loose from their hold on a rail.

"A lot of these land fellows, they try not to be sick. You can see their faces changing color and them swallowing and eyes sticking out. There were this German fellow; he'd come all the way from other side, and he were, like, he were, well, very tough. There were nothing we could tell him. It were a very cold day, and rough, and he stood out in the wind, very tough. We were watching him. He got quieter and quieter. Father, he said, 'I think he's going, I think he's going.' But he held on, and he held on, and he looked ready to die, and we just waited. Then he went to the side and Father, and the other boys, they laughed."

There was no rancor in Sturge's voice.

"It be hard not to be sick on the longliner," he said.

When the sun did appear, it had none of the oranges and reds that heralded so many summer dawns on this coast. It was a savage white. But for a hint of warmth from it, I might have felt it was made of ice. Suddenly, the sea was different, hard and bright. Scores of shearwaters twisted across the track of the sun, black silhouettes, like bats in brilliant moonlight.

"It looks good," Arthur Sturge said. "If the wind be from the north now, the sun would be red. But clear like that, means a good day."

The bellowing engines pushed us on beyond the dawn, which became a hot light burning into our eyeballs. One by one, the men disappeared below, leaving Uncle Jacob at the wheel. I felt the impact caused by only one hour's sleep. Perhaps I might bunk down for a couple of hours myself. I went down a vertical ladder into the roaring forecastle.

The men were asleep. Each had less than eighteen inches of berth, yet they maintained their positions. One man lay on his face, cheek pressed hard against the wooden edge of the bunk, his arms bent up and ahead, holding his body steady. Another man wedged his head behind a bunk support and twisted his legs to give his body reflex leverage against the curve of the boat's bows. The men were still, as deep in sleep as if they were dead, impervious to the racket of the engines three feet away behind a thin bulkhead, unconscious of the savage motion of the hull. The heat, the motion, the smell of a fried meal on the wood stove drove me topside. I sat in the sun alone and waited for the Funks.

Uncle Jacob was in my thoughts. At his age, sixty-seven, he was a perfect example of the old, superstitious attitude toward the Funk Islands. For more than two hundred years, the Funks were considered haunted. It was easy to see why: the isolation of the islands, the howling noises during storms, the ships wrecked there. The islands might be haunted by a fisherman who was buried there many years ago, his bones placed under a pile of granite slabs. During a storm a few years ago, his skull pan was washed out of the grave, and it was chivvied around the island for a couple of years. One of Uncle Jacob's boys had once suggested, perhaps with a hint of humor, that the skull pan might make a good boat bailer; but nobody was game to pick it up.

The Funks symbolized danger and death at sea. Probably they were plundered by the Vikings a thousand years ago. The Beothuk Indians certainly got bird and egg stores there for a thousand years before the coming of the Vikings. Various races of Eskimo must have visited the islands, on and off, for thousands of years.

During the days of waiting at Valleyfield, I had noticed how much the Funks were on Uncle Jacob's mind. He would become suddenly reflective, and I would hear him mutter: "Ay, de Funks, de Funks," as if repeating some half-forgotten memory to himself.

Like all old Newfoundland men, his memories were becoming stronger with age, as his effectiveness as the family leader diminished with a young family pushing up under him.

The Sturge boys referred to him as "Farder," in a genial bellow that could be heard a hundred yards away. He got shouted out during the fishing season for turning too sharply to starboard, for failing to see another fisherman's net, for going astern too slowly, for going ahead too sharply. He stood at the big wheel, jabbing and yanking at the controls (a length of knotted rope which provided an uneasy link with the two massive diesels underfoot), and he could be heard mumbling under his breath while, aft and forrard, came a mounting roar of "Farder!"

His good humor was unending. He expected to be bawled at. His boys knew nothing of the days of sail, of hands frozen to oars, of schooners leaning dangerously in arctic winds, and only a man's imperfect memory to know the shoals, the islands and the tides.

He grinned at me. "So you're goin' to the Funks!" he shouted. "Oh, aye, you're a'goin' to the Funks. Oh aaaaaar!"

He reached a bucket over the side and scooped up a brimming load of water, slipped the straps of his thigh boots of his shoulders, defecated, and hurled the water overboard.

"Oh, it be a lonely place up there. At night, in the lea of the island, with them turrs rushing and roaring, you wonder how such an island can be, stuck out there in the middle of the ocean."

He went back into the wheelhouse.

"Yair," Jacob said. "It be a sight you'll not forget."

We sailed for an hour.

Uncle Jacob's blunt finger stabbed ahead. "We be steerin' for her!" he said. An iceberg bulked on the horizon. It seemed big as a cathedral, and as I sought to establish perspective, I thought it must be hundreds of feet high. As we sailed on, the berg grew bigger with astonishing speed. I thought I must be experiencing some peculiar optical illusion. I watched, puzzled. The iceberg was triangular and thrust up a tall pinnacle of ice into the air. But no, it was square; no, not square, rectangular; well, not really rectangular, it was triangular again, and growing taller every minute.

Avalon Sturge came into the wheelhouse, took the wheel, and we watched the iceberg.

"See her roll," he said.

Then I realized the iceberg was heaving slowly back and forth like a great stricken animal. We passed within a thousand feet of it, yet its movement was imperceptible, indicated only by its endlessly changing profile.

We ground on north among a thousand shearwaters cutting across our bows.

I had seen icebergs from Flowers Island and at other points along the coast, but I was scarcely prepared for what I saw now, as the sun rose and the air cleared. Icebergs stood along the horizon, great buildings of a secret arctic city. I watched and was puzzled again by a strangely shaped iceberg, very tall and slender—or was it an iceberg? It disappeared; rather, it *dematerialized*, and left me staring. Had I seen anything, or was it an illusion? Another slender column appeared and hung, opaque and real, before it, too, faded slowly. My eyes ran along the horizon, settled on one iceberg after another. The tall columns rose between the bergs, stabbing up at a score of points at once. I counted more than thirty columns, rising and fading, superimposing themselves on their own fading images. Avalon Sturge was pleased. "Yar! Whales. Dey're comin' back."

The arctic whale populations are building up again following their decimation by whalers throughout the seventeenth, eighteenth, and nineteenth centuries. Fishermen, though they do not hunt whales, find the return of the big mammals a good and satisfactory thing, palpable proof of the old stories about their size and power.

We had sailed three and a half hours. All the men came on deck and gathered in the wheelhouse and in the bows.

"Us'll see her soon," Uncle Jacob said.

Suddenly, one of the men up forrard cried out:

"We're a'goin' to the island, we're a'goin' to the island!" The men grinned like kids. The island was pulling us, drawing us north. We no longer needed the Funk wind blowing on our backs. We shared the excitement of our arrival. The men had made my purpose their own.

"Now I see her," Uncle Jacob said.

"Yair," Arthur said. "That's her, all right."

I saw nothing. I used binoculars, but the horizon was empty. An old sealing captain once told me he could see seals twenty miles away if there were clouds because he could "see pictures of them on the clouds." But there were no clouds here.

"Now I see her," said Willie.

"I see her too," Perce said.

The horizon remained empty.

Cyril turned from the bows and shouted, "I can't see the island, I can't see the island, I can't see the island!"

I thought he had gone out of his head.

"Now I can see the other island," Arthur said. "You see her there, just to the left."

The horizon remained empty.

"Now you can see the big island," Uncle Jacob said. I saw nothing. We sailed for another five minutes.

"There she are," Arthur said with satisfaction. Anybody could see it now, he was saying.

Cyril was in a state. "I can never see the island, I'm never going to see the island!"

He threw himself on the deck and kicked his big boots and bellowed with rage.

"I can't see her!"

The others were grinning, and I realized it was a joke for all of them. Cyril stood up and grinned with them.

"His glasses are no damn good," Arthur said.

At that moment, I saw the island, so big and clear I wondered why I had not spotted it before. We sailed through a scattering of shearwaters and fulmars.

I looked through the binoculars and saw the air above the island streaming with the movement of hundreds of thousands of birds.

7

The Island of Auks

ARTHUR STURGE was caught in an immortal moment, straining back on his oar as he moved the heavy dory toward Funk Island. This was the last lunge of the journey; the long-liner heaved behind us; Uncle Jacob had bellowed his final exhortation of good luck.

I saw the island close up as I glanced over Sturge's shoulder, and I knew I was duplicating the experience of a thousand men before me. From the boat it seemed incredible that such a stream of humanity—explorers, Indians, sealers, whalers, codfishermen—had ever reached this lonely place. Yet the island, and its auks, had drawn them as it was drawing me.

The island was a blank wall of rock, thirty feet high, suave and bland, and topped by a thin, fast-moving frieze of murres who, presumably, were anxiously watching our boat. I have read about a moment of truth, even written about it, but not until I was in this dory, in this place, did I really understand what it meant. It was the final throw of the dice. Would we be able to land?

"Hard to say. Them waves is risin' high. . . ."

I looked toward the island and saw the water pitching, silent and ominous, up the blank rock. I had come
this far, but now I could think only of being capsized—
dashed against the rocks or maimed under the boat's
keel. I had already talked to a dozen men who had
traveled thousands of miles only to be turned back at
this point.

I sat in the back of the dory, carried forward by the
momentum of a determination long sustained. In a
moment, the boat was rising and falling against the rock
face on six-foot waves.

"Get up front," Arthur Sturge said.

He eased the boat toward the rock. Willie hunched
in the bows. At the peak of a wave, he jumped, grabbed
at the rock face, and clung. I could see that the rock
was gouged with handholds into which my fingers must
fit as I jumped.

"Arl roight!" Arthur shouted.

Willie now had his back to the rock; he was facing
me so that he might try to seize me if I fell. The boat
rose and wobbled at its peak; I jumped, hit the rocks,
and felt my fingers slip into the grooves. As I clung
there, I realized the grooves were man-made. Of course.
Other men had met the same problem. Of course they
had done something about it. These grooves into which
my fingers fitted so neatly might have been cut in
Drake's time, or before, when the Beothuk Indians came
to plunder the island; or had they been cut by Eskimos,
a thousand years before Christ?

Muscles knotted, and I strained upward. The problems of landing on Funk Island have remained unchanged. Rockets to the moon and the splitting of the atom mean nothing when it comes to landing on Funk Island. The equation for success is constant: an open boat with a skillful oarsman and a man willing to jump.

Willie had disappeared over the top of the rock while I was still absorbed in finding hand- and footholds in rock slippery with algae and bird excrement. I mounted the crest of the rock and Funk Island spread out, an explosion of sight, sound, and smell. I saw, but I did not see; I saw dark masses of murres in the distance; I saw curtains of buzzing kittiwakes interposing themselves like thousands of pretty white butterflies; I saw rolling hummocks of bare rock. But it was the sound that came to me first. We walked forward over intransigent, bare granite, and the sound swelled like thunder. A literate biologist has described it as "a rushing of waters," but that description does not satisfy poet or artist. It is orchestral, if a million players can be imagined: rich, sensuous, hypnotic.

When we came to the edge of the first great concourse of birds, perhaps two hundred thousand of them staining the rock densely black and white, the orchestral analogy became even more vivid because I could hear, among those thousands of voices, rippling spasms of pathos and melancholy—Brahmsian. The adult birds cried *ehr-ehr-ehr*, crescendo, diminuendo, gushes of emotion. The cries of the flying birds—and there were

thousands in the air—swelled and faded in haunting harmony as they passed low overhead. Buried in this
amalgam of voices were the piping screams of the
young murres, sounds so piercing they hurt the ear.

We moved around the periphery of the murres. With
every step, I was conscious of new expansions in the
scope of sound. A sibilant undertone to the massive main
theme was faintly discernible, the sound of innumerable
wings beating: *flacka-flacka-flacka-flacka*. Wings struck
each other—*clack, clack, clack*—as birds, flying in thick
layers, collided in mid-air. Then another buried sound,
a submelody, a counterpoint: *gaggla-gaggla-gaggla*. The
gannets were hidden somewhere among the murre
hordes. Other sounds were reduced to minutiae in the
uproar: the thin cries of herring gulls, the rasping moans
of kittiwakes hovering high overhead.

I had been on the island an hour and only now was
I really registering the sound of it.

Next, overwhelmingly, came real vision. The murres
were massed so thickly they obscured the ground. The
birds stood shoulder to shoulder, eyeball to eyeball. In
places, they were so densely packed that if one bird
stretched or flapped her wings, she sent a sympathetic
spasm rippling away from her on all sides.

All life was in constant, riotous motion. Murre heads
wavered and darted; wings beat; birds landed clumsily
among the upraised heads of their comrades; birds took
off and thrashed passageways through the birds ahead
of them, knocking them down. Chicks ran from adult to

adult; eggs rolled across bare rock, displaced by kicking feet.

The murres heeded me, yet they did not. I approached them and a rising roar of protest sounded, a concentration of the general uproar, which seemed not directed at me at all but at the outrage of intrusion. I walked away from them and the roar died instantly.

The sun was well up, a brilliant star in an azure sky, and I walked to the quiet shore, away from the main masses of murres. Willie had disappeared into a gully. Perhaps I needed time to assimilate. But there was no time. The multiple dimensions of the sight came pouring in. The air streamed with birds coming at me. I threw up my hands, shouted at them, but the shout was lost, ineffectual, not causing a single bird to swerve or otherwise acknowledge me.

At least a hundred thousand birds were aloft at once. They circled the island endlessly, like fighter bombers making strafing runs on a target, flying the full length of the island, then turning out to sea and sweeping back offshore to begin another run. They came on relentlessly and the sky danced with them.

This was not, I realized, the hostile reaction of individual birds who saw their nests threatened. Instead, the murres were a tribe of animals resisting a threat to their island. Individually, they intimidated nothing. Collectively, they emanated power and strength. I looked into a thousand cold eyes and felt chill, impersonal hostility in the air.

I climbed to the top of a ridge and looked down the length of the island, looked into the masses of birds hurtling toward me, looked down to the grounded hordes, a living, writhing backbone of murres, murres, murres. Then, after the visual shock came the olfactory impact.

The smell of Funk Island is the smell of death. It is probably the source of the island's name, which in various languages means "to steam," "to create a great stench," "to smoke"; it may also mean "fear." The island certainly smells ghastly. No battlefield could ever concentrate such a coalition of dead and dying.

A change of wind brought the smell to us, choking, sickening. As I walked down a slope and out of the force of the wind, the air clotted with the smell. In a hollow at the bottom of the slope, it had collected in such concentration that I gagged and my throat constricted. The fishermen *knew* the smell was poisonous. Uncle Jacob Sturge had told me how one fisherman who tried to run through the concentration of birds was nearly gassed unconscious.

The smell of Funk Island comes from a combination of corruption. There are no scavengers, except bacteria, so dead bodies lie where they have fallen. The debris of a million creatures has nowhere to go. Eggs by the scores of thousands lie everywhere, so that I could not see which were being brooded, which were rotten. In one small gully, unwanted or untended eggs had been kicked together in a one hundred foot driftline by the constantly moving feet of the birds.

The smell of the island came in diminishing waves as the sea breeze died and the heat rose from the rocks. A ripple of explosions fled away among a nearby concentration of birds. I listened; the sound was manlike. It reminded me of a popgun I had used when I was a boy. From a nearby hill packed with murres, another flurry of explosions, then single shots haphazardly firing all around me. If the smell of the island needed an exemplifying sound, this was it. The explosions were the sound of rotten eggs bursting in the growing heat.

I walked, while the smell gathered in my nostrils and took on various identities. It was the thin, sour smell of bird excrement: acidic, astringent, more than a hundred tons of it splashed on the island every day. Underlying that smell was the stench of the rotting fish which lay everywhere after being vomited up by the parent murres but not eaten by the nestlings. The smell was of putrescence, of oil, of fish, and of an indescribable other thing: the stench of a million creatures packed together in a small place.

I walked halfway down the length of the island, a distance of perhaps five hundred feet, but my progress was slow because of the difficulty I had in assimilating everything I saw.

In my mind were scraps of history. I was thinking, for instance, of how Newfoundland's ancient Indians, the Beothuks, camped in a gulch when they were on bird- and egg-hunting expeditions; of how, until recently, the gulch was an archaeological repository of old knives, spoons, belaying pins, and broken pots, testifying to more than two hundred years of exploitation of the island by hunters of meat, oil, eggs, and feathers.

Willie appeared on a far ridge. He was standing at the edge of Indian Gulch. I walked toward him along the rim of a concourse of murres. A feeble spring flowed into the gulch and created a small pond, which was also fed by the sea during heavy swells. Sea water belched up into it through a narrow crack in the rock. Into this pond poured a ceaseless flow of excrement, coughed-up fish, bodies, rotten eggs, and live nestlings. By midsummer, the water was mucid, pea-green, fermenting, almost bubbling with corruption.

The murres were not distressed by this putrid mess; as Willie walked along the top of the gulch, hundreds of them dropped down to the water and floated. Suddenly, the pond was roiled into green foam as a group of birds took off. Their departure triggered another flight, which because murres fly poorly, was a failure. The birds crashed on top of each other or piled into heaps along the steep banks. This drew a sympathetic flight from murres perched precariously on the cliffs and a cloud of birds took off. Their departure sent eggs and nestlings spilling off the cliffs into the water.

But on Funk Island, nothing matters. Death is nothing. Life is nothing. Chaos is order. Order is a mystery. Time is meaningless. The deep-throated roar of the colony cries out to a heedless sky. The human observer, cowed by its primitive energy, by its suggestion of the unnameable, stumbles on blindly.

As I walked, I examined my growing sense of reality and sought a guidepost to what it all meant. I had thought (an hour before? two hours? it was nearer to four hours) that a sweep of Brahmsian rhetoric could describe the island. Already, the image was obsolete. Now, I felt a mechanistic sense, Prokofievian, an imperative monotone, the sound of Mars. The struggling, homuncular forms piled together in such utter, inhuman chaos denied any ordered view of the universe.

I had to wonder whether a poet had preceded me to the island; or did the island have a counterpart elsewhere? De la Mare's disgust at the massacre?

> And silence fell: the rushing sun
> Stood still in paths of heat,
> Gazing in waves of horror on
> The dead about my feet.

It was nearly noon, and sun flames reached for the island and scorched it. I was enervated, but I was also recovering normal sensibility, which brought me *details* of the life of the murre colony. Everywhere I looked now, young murres looked back. In places, they were packed thirty and forty together among the adults. There is only one word to describe them and it is not in any dictionary. They are murrelings: tiny, rotund, dusky balls of fluff with the most piercing voices ever given a young bird. Their piping screams must be essential for them to assert themselves above the roar of the adults. How else could they identify themselves to their parents? Yet, bafflement grew as I watched them. One murreling in that featureless mass of birds was infinitely smaller than one needle in a stack of hay. How contact is kept with the parent birds remains a mystery of biology.

Warned by the scope of destruction in the colony, I was not surprised to find that the murrelings were expendable. Life moves to and from the colony at high speed. A murreling fell from a rock, bounced into an evil puddle, and was trampled by a throng of adults. Hearing screams from a rock I disengaged a murreling jammed in a crevice, looked down, saw a mass of fluffy bodies wedged deeper in the crevice. Murrelings fell from cliffs into the sea, rose and floated in foam, screaming. Murrelings lay dead among pustular eggs; they lay in heaps and windrows in olivaceous puddles.

I knew from murre literature that the murrelings often became shocked by prolonged rain and died by the thousands. That, in the context of this island, was not surprising. An *individual* death was shocking. Willie had walked back up the other side of the island and we met at the edge of a group of murres. Willie groaned.

"I don't feel well," he said, rolling his eyes in mock nausea.

As he spoke, I looked over his shoulder in horror. In the middle of the murre mass, standing on slightly higher ground, was a group of gannets. These birds, though inferior in number, occupied the best territory. Though dominant, they seemed to have an amicable relationship with the murres. In places, murres and gannets were mixed together; murrelings gathered around gannets as though they were murres.

A gannet on a nest had reached down casually for one of these nearby murrelings, and as I watched, up-ended it and swallowed the struggling youngster. It was not the sight of such casual destruction that was shocking; it was the sound of the murreling dying.

It screamed when it was seized by the gannet's beak, which was bigger than the murreling's entire body. It screamed as it was hoisted into the air. Horrifyingly, it screamed loudest as it was being swallowed. The gannet, though a big, powerful bird, had to swallow hard to get the murreling down. Its neck writhed and its beak gaped and all the time the awful screams of the murreling came up out of the gannet's throat. The cries became fainter and fainter.

"Horrible," Willie said. "Oi never gets used to it."

The roar of the birds became a lamentation, a collusion of agony and sorrow. The flying creatures seemed to be in streaming retreat. Why *that* murreling and not any of the others still around at the feet of the gannet? If gannets really relished murre flesh, surely they would quickly wipe out all the murrelings near them. But they do not.

It was now afternoon and the sun plashed white and pitiless light on rock. For some time, I had been aware of a growing disorientation. I took a picture to the east, seventy thousand birds; to the west, one hundred thousand; in the air, twenty thousand. The noise, the smell, the screams, the corpses, the green puddles, pushed bonily into my chest. I fumbled with film but could not decide how to reload the camera or, indeed, remember what setting to use, or how to release the shutter.

"Oi t'ink oi'll go and sit behind dat rock," Willie said. "Oi goes funny in de head after a while here."

Uncle Jacob had mentioned that the island could drive a man mad. I was being sickened by the pressure of it. Once, in Australia, I watched men systematically kill several hundred thousand rabbits they had penned against a fence. The steady thocking of cudgels hammering rabbit skulls continued hour after hour, eventually dulling the eye and diminishing the hearing. On Funk Island, my observing sense was losing its ability to see and to record.

I sought release in reverie and walked, half-conscious of what I was doing, toward an incongruous green field that lay alone in the middle of the island. Its bareness suggested another place of personal memory, and an association of ideas. My ancestors were Scottish and fought the English at Culloden. When I went to Culloden, two hundred years after the battle, I was overwhelmed by those long, sinister mounds of mass burial of the clans.

This Funk Island field was also a midden of slain creatures. It was a great natural-history site, as significant to an ornithologist as Ashurbanipal's palace would be to an archaeologist. Here, generations of flightless great auks had flocked to breed after eight months of oceanic wandering. Their occupancy built up soil. Here, also, they were slain throughout the eighteenth century until they became extinct, probably early in the nineteenth.

A puffin bolted out of the ground ahead and flipped a bone from her burrow entrance as she left. I knelt and clawed a handful of bones out of the burrow. I saw other burrows, bones spilling out of them as though they were entrances to a disorderly catacomb.

This was not fantasy. These were great-auk bones, still oozing out of the earth nearly a hundred and fifty years after the last bird had gone. The bones permeated the ground under my feet; puffins dug among them and kicked them aside to find graveyard sanctuary. Life in the midst of death.

All at once, walking across bare rock, the murres well distant, I felt a release. Willie was not in sight; the longliner was off fishing somewhere. The granite underfoot changed texture, became a desert I had walked, then a heath, a moor I had tramped, and eventually, all the bare and empty places of earth I had ever known. I felt the presence of friends and heard their voices. But something was wrong. Some were still friends but others had closed, deceitful faces. Inhibition and self-deception fell away; flushes of hate and love passed as the faces moved back and forth. Forgotten incidents came to mind. What was happening?

Uncle Jacob's voice: "A man could go mad on the Funks."

This was enough. I turned toward the shore, to the *Doris and Lydia*, which had appeared from nowhere. Willie leaped eagerly from his place of refuge behind a rock. The roar of the murres receded. I imagined the island empty during much of the long year, naked as a

statue against the silent hiss of mist coming out of the
Labrador Current, or the thunder of an Atlantic gale
piling thirty-foot waves up the sides of the island.

"She be a sight to see in the winter," Uncle Benny
had said.

The seasons of millennia switched back and forth.
The island suffocated in the original gases of earth:
argon, radon, krypton, xenon, neon. The island disappeared in yellow fog, and water slid down its sides.
The island was a corpse, dead a million years, its surface
liquefied, with rot running into its granite intestines.
The island festered, and rivulets of pus coursed down
its sides. The island was death. The island was life.

Only in retrospect could the island become real.
Later, I was to return to the island and actually live on
it in order to turn my disbelief into lasting memory.
Willie moved parallel to me, jumping from rock to rock
and displacing a fluttering canopy of kittiwakes. He was
a different man now as he met me at the landing site,
beaming and lighthearted.

"So dat's de Funks, eh?" he said, and he was proud
that I had seen it.

In the boat below us, Arthur and Cyril smiled.
Arthur was relaxed now, in contrast to his silent, absorbed intensity when he was trying to get me to the
island, and on it. Both men, and Willie, poised at the
top of the cliff, were caught for a moment by the camera,
like toreros who have survived a bloody afternoon and
will hear the bugles again tomorrow.

With a final look over my shoulder at the silently fleeing birds, I slid down the cliff to the boat and Funk Island became a part of the history of my life.

8

A Stillness at Bonaventure

A T DAWN, the view east from the great cliffs of Bonaventure Island strikes into the heart. Two hundred square miles of ocean sprawl below the observer. Just before sunrise, the water glows with light that radiates out of the air. Lines of steel-blue clouds run along the horizon, their bottom edges fired by the unseen sun.

Sea birds hover and dart across the oceanic canvas, Brueghelian in its endless moving detail. Birds leap from the cliffs and hang in space, going nowhere. Cries, cast into such a void, are multilayered and it is easy to imagine, at least for me, that they acquire colors as they descend to land. I hear the gannets, soaring highest, gargling in imperial purple cadences. I hear the kittiwakes ululating in bursts of yellow. Gulls shout, black and white. In the background, murres cry a purring gray *continuo*.

After the experience of Funk Island, I felt drained. It had been an ultimate. Why go on? Surely everything would be anticlimactic now. Rain, fog, and wind deepened my distaste for traveling. Funk Island suggested that I return home, sobered by a vision of the future.

Then I became friends with a man who was making a quick flight in a small plane to the other side of the Gulf of St. Lawrence. Did I want a ride? This, I knew, would take me near the island of Bonaventure at the tip of the Gaspé Peninsula. It would take me five hundred miles from Funk Island and momentarily interrupt my scheme of travel. In effect, it would give me a breathing spell.

The cliffs of Bonaventure run for more than a mile along the eastward side of the island, two hundred feet high at their tallest point. Their vertical face is cut, split, and broken into lines, crevices, and holes. About two hundred thousand birds nest in this structure each summer. Every foothold is occupied. The kittiwakes nest on any ledge more than three inches wide. The murres have colonized a cliff cave. Above them all are the regal gannets, who occupy the slopes at the top of the cliffs. They are pushing their nesting area into the forest, slowly killing the trees by the density of their occupation.

As I watch, the sun appears.

I find it impossible now to watch a sunrise without recalling Bonaventure. The sun is the eye of God; the cliffs are an altar. An accusing shaft of light jumps across the sea, strikes the cliffs, and the island shudders. Surely there is no light west of the island; it must all stop here. The gannets are red, pink, white.

Bonaventure, for a mystic reason, is a place for contemplation. It is inhabited; but it permits the traveler to take a dozen steps and be alone. It is close to the mainland, yet it allows him to find varying degrees of solitude. Its atmosphere is, in the end, subjective. A man from Brooklyn once told me it was the most boring place he had ever visited.

I landed on a bumpy hay field in the early evening and within minutes the mainland village of Percé was dwindling behind me as a fishing boat pushed me toward Bonaventure. Though the sky threatened rain, I set off immediately from the western side of the island for the gannet cliffs, along a winding, rutted track which plunged through spruce trees. At such an hour, the woods were silent, except for the tisping of hidden birds and sudden bursts of late song. On the track, it was almost dark. My only reassurance that I was not too late to see the gannets was an occasional glimpse of the sky, still blue and bright, through the trees. The track was uphill most of the way; the exertion of the walk and the excitement of the new experience which lay just ahead made my heart thump. When I stopped, I heard its hollow boom in the still forest.

Near the end of the track, after the low peak of the island had been reached and passed, the forest thinned. Straight ahead, and caught in the last light of the sinking sun, about a hundred gannets appeared in a rift among the trees. They flew with the absolute distinction of their kind, running through the air as if they were on rails, a smooth, fluid rush of motion that did not rock, tip, or yaw.

I ran down the slope into the open and saw the

gannet colony spread before me: a narrow army of squatting birds so densely packed over their eggs and nestlings they whitened the cliff top. Some sat inches from the edge. Above, aerialists cruised; cross-shaped, pure white with touches of yellow on their heads. They flew, I realized, for no reason except the joy of flight. They coasted on a soft wind and were warmed and colored by the western sun.

All roads lead to Bonaventure's cliffs. In the world of natural history, this island is one of the seven wonders, yet few people really see it. Each year, thousands of tourists pass the cliffs in launches to witness the external reality of the island. I have traveled with them, watching them. They sit, dull-eyed and uncomprehending.

Birds?

Cliffs?

Hmmm.

The launches disappear, the people are swallowed up in the mainland, and I am left on the island.

The internal island is hidden and yields to imagination after its cliffs have been climbed and its forest felt at night. At rare times, the island releases a hint of its secret self. Stillness grows out of the ground; expectation grows and lingers and caresses the senses. The mind ranges in search of a similar peace in other times and other places. I feel it: an Australian desert at midnight, a tropical forest after monsoon rains.

I sat on grassed slopes on the western side of the island and felt stillness substantial enough to weigh in

my hand. I waited there throughout a morning. At last
I had it. The stillness was the *sound* of the island retreating into the past. Bonaventure has been waiting a long
time to rid itself of men. Its time is nearly come.

There were once forty families on the island. There
are now fewer than half a dozen. Some buildings remain
and anticipate destruction. They have weathered a silver
color and gleam quietly. Ancient footprints track the
sparrow-filled grass but lead only to broken shutters.

I lay and dreamed and felt other areas of the stillness. The island is a mile offshore. Could the mainland
ever spill over into this quiet place? I watched the sun
race past the island and flood the farther shore. Windows
gleamed there, but on the island, it was a painter's light,
reflected and subtle. A Rembrandt highlight? No. More
silver than gold. It ran along every leaf and grass stalk
to reveal objects with lithographic clarity. A cock
crowed; his cry was made of silver too.

The mainland awoke. The silver light shattered; the
cock died. Shouts, blatting horns, tires squealing, a shot
—sounds made in hell and created by madmen. For one
unhappy second, I saw chewing gum, hubcaps, cameras,
bleached hair, dollar bills, spitting. Then the infernal
vision died as the sun appeared over my shoulder and
the cool serenity of the island shut out the sound of the
mainland.

When it is calm at Bonaventure (which is not often)
the evening gives way to sensuous dusk. It grows among
the grass stems, rises and enfolds the watcher. This dusk
is as special to the night as the silver light is to the

island's days. I stood on the shore that evening and looked toward Percé Rock, a black shape cut out of the glowing west. Impulsively, I stripped off my clothes and took to the water. It was cold fire, but my imagination warmed me. I swam offshore through calm water and put my face half underwater to let the nacreous colors of the stricken sunset wash into my eyes. I felt the cold suddenly, but instead of freezing me, it sent me sliding through the water like a fish. I was weightless, exhilarated. As a sea creature, I was able to watch my fellow creatures without intrusion. This was a special time for the gulls. Several hundred black silhouettes collected on the lustrous water between me and the dusky mainland. Eventually, they settled around me and I became part of their twilight world.

At this moment, this second, this fragment of time, I was alone in watching this scene. The sun disappeared; the water was a paten of polished ebony; Percé Rock, a sepulcher with a single glowing eye where light shone through a hole in its body, a million years ahead of modern art. Ripples spread away from my chin and gulls clotted suddenly like a spray of bats. They settled with weird cries. I kicked forward and watched the island become a part of the night.

The blackness of the sea was not absolute; it left me free to see and to feel. Were the gulls still floating nearby? Or had they gone to safer roosts ashore? Would any bird dare to spend a night afloat where fish and seals and killer whales prowled?

As if in answer to my thoughts, I heard a movement.

It was a whisper of water but was not like the rippling of a rising fish school. This sound had a throaty timbre. Suddenly, I was badly chilled. A large body was passing close by. I held my breath and felt my cowardly legs weaken. I strained to hear another sound. I seemed to see the hazy outlines of the creature's form as it swam between me and the island in graceful, undulating, whalelike movements. The image, or delusion, was so precise I waited for the sound of its surfacing. The whisper of water came again. The creature dived and was gone toward Percé Rock. The night pressed in from all sides. The spell of the evening was destroyed, and I butterflied to shore with as much noise and speed as I could manage.

When I was young, I was a night prowler. I would steal from my bedroom and walk the familiar day places now become foreign, exciting, and disturbing in the dark. I became familiar with the night world of owls, weasels, cats, rabbits, hares, frogs, worms, and beetles. Because man is almost blind at night, his other senses take over in his perception of truth. A squawling cry of pain from a hedgerow—what does it mean? A sudden trill of exquisite song—what bird is that? The skin is touched with cool suede as a night wind brushes past and the scent of a midnight flower (can that be?) drifts into the nostrils. The night is solitude.

I had experienced the fringe of night at Bonaventure; I wanted to pass beyond it. The eastern cliffs of the island are a nesting territory for petrels, swallowlike sea birds who, though diurnal, only dare to come to their burrows in darkness. The night walk across the island took me under thick trees where the moonlight, piercing them, spilled like smoky liquid into the undergrowth. This was a third stage of solitude offered by Bonaventure. First, there had been the withdrawal from the mainland to the island. Second had been the withdrawal from the people. And now, the retreat into night was the third isolation; it would shut out the real world completely.

The track reached its summit and began the downward slope which led to the cliffs. I passed out of the forest and new vision came, the negative of an under-exposed film. Every detail was dark with a suggestion of reality. The moon was lost behind clouds, but its light tracked the sea. I saw the silhouettes of gannets, the glowing edges of grass and leaves and branches. A mutter of concern growled among the birds.

Aggla-aggla-aggla-aggla.

I walked along the cliffs parallel to their narrow colony as the moon slid into view. It lit the petrels. A bird appeared in the moon's track, cutting along with the lithe urgency of a swallow, swerving back and forth as though trying to avoid invisible objects in mid-air. Another petrel dropped down to follow and the two birds shot along in chase. Other petrels appeared in the distance, swinging back and forth across the lighted track: a phantasmagoria suggesting winged creatures but so dim, so fleet, that I expected them to vanish any second. I walked through long grass and among low scrub, the moon's reflection moving silently beside me, until I came to the petrels' nesting territory. I lay down to watch.

Any gathering of petrels is memorable, but on these cliffs it was as though I were among them, hundreds of feet in mid-air. They sped back and forth over their territory, and their bright cries came from overhead and from far beneath me as they came out of the sea and mounted the cliffs.

After hours of listening to sly movements in the grass as the petrels found their burrows near me, I was shocked by a sudden, percussive sound, like a man slapping his hand hard against his trousered thigh; a voice squealed. A steady, grinding noise followed.

The violence and proximity of the sound made me shiver, and for an hour I strained for a clue to its identity. The sound came again, hollow this time, and farther away. There was no cry, no grinding noise. Then I saw a tense, lithe body outlined in the reflection of the moon. Its head pointed upward, its attitude expressed leashed power awaiting release. It moved, sharply, from one fixed position to another.

The fox was reaching for petrels, adjusting himself as he watched their speedy flight and listened to the rush of their wings sounding on all sides. For long seconds, a petrel hovered over his head; the fox strained upward, yearning. He jumped. Petrel and fox came together; the slapping sound again, the steady, grinding noise again.

As the moon brightened, the fox divined my inimical presence and slid away. I walked back to the other side of the island through a forest buzzing with owl calls.

The drowsy stillness of Bonaventure anoints the nerve ends as it stretches away into the future. Chips of stained-glass flowers hide behind a sagging house. The sky pales and that silver light makes a compact with everything it touches: I will make you, leaf, into an abstraction which man cannot paint or photograph or write about. I will transform you, tree, into a complex of detail that makes you invisible as a tree. You are, first, the delicacy of your detail. Second, you are a tree.

The light is married to the stillness—perhaps they are the same thing—but I am sure it never reaches the mainland. I see it in the silver-tipped wing feathers of hovering gulls who respect the silence and do not utter their customary cries of reproof at my presence.

One morning, I awoke in darkness and listened. Silence. I walked to the edge of the forest and listened. Silence. I turned inland in the direction of the cliffs, thinking of the silence *there*, the light *there*, at the beginning of this day. But instead of walking through the forest toward the cliffs, I found myself being taken along the shore, as though I must circumnavigate the island.

The first touch of light came when I was struggling through a thicket. Vague white forms whisked overhead and gulls spoke intimately. I thought I was alone, but as I let myself down a rock face toward the water, I felt a watching presence. A score of silent boats, all pointed at me, were spread out of sight into the sea gloom. Nothing moved. No fisherman stirred. The fishing boats slept in the refuge of the lea shore while they awaited . . . what?

The light grew quickly; the boats leaped out of the gloom. Above them, a double stream of gannets passed beyond, one stream heading south, the other, north toward the island. Early as it was, the gannets already had found good fishing. I slipped to the edge of the water among huge, rounded rocks.

The light grew and I was drawn along the rocks. This morning, calm, warm, silent, was probably the only day in this year, in this decade, when sea and air were so calm and a man might stand below the cliffs and watch. The rocks curved up; the cliff rose straight; the horizon glowed in notification of the sunrise.

By the time I came within sight of the colonized cliffs, I was wet and panting from a dozen plunges into the water. The porcelain sea did not move until I was in it. Then, gigantic spasms lifted me, deceptively, slowly, and elbow and thigh scraped against rock.

Eventually, I stood on a ledge twelve inches wide and faced east. At my back, two hundred feet of vertical rock; before me, three thousand miles of uninterrupted sea, then Ireland; above me, two hundred thousand birds. The air was not silver here, no subtlety about it. It was pale blue, washed with salt and foam, and its acrid flavor burned my nostrils.

This was the matrix of the island. I looked up to see heads craning out at me; I heard the split and splat of falling excrement. The cries of the birds exploded sharply against rock. Small stones fell, skittered, plopped. An egg curved down and burst, yellow. A young murre, tiny and immaculate in black-and-white uniform, dropped near me and was killed.

In this moment of absolute, primal isolation, myself unreachable, and unknown, the sun rose. Liquid fire, heat, blazing red sea, blinding . . .

I shouted.

From the birds came an answering roar, and they broke away from the cliffs in clouds.

I shouted again.

Debris fell, kittiwakes swarmed; the sun rose, a merciless inquisitor. Murres bolted; gannets shouted inquiries; I was pinned against the rock.

But even while the sun hurtled upward, revolution gathered in the north. Black clouds fled south together. Distantly, the water flattened under the first finger of the squall awaited by the fishermen, still asleep in their safe bunks. The sun went out in a hiss of mist and I was left alone, chilled and frightened, in contemplation of my folly.

Should I retrace my route under the cliffs in flight from the storm? Or should I keep moving forward, toward the squall? I had the feeling that the cliffs were not as steep or as high a short distance ahead. I took to the water and swam. Cormorants raced the wind, black arrows a foot off the water. Gannets glided inward and disappeared. The kittiwakes were silent and had settled.

A group of murres came low across the water, zoomed up, and shot into a hole in the cliffs.

As I swam and scrambled over rock, the cliffs became more broken and less steep. I was climbing when the squall struck, and had a good grip on the rocks. I climbed among birds, who ignored me. The kittiwakes pressed themselves and their nestlings against the streaming rock. Gannets on ledges raised their beaks to parry cascades of falling water. I climbed against a rock face polluted by the acrid smell of excrement being flushed away by the rushing water. I scrambled over one last smooth rock and headed inland.

Later, sitting among spruces with the rain abruptly stopped, I looked into sunlight that glowed unexpectedly in the black overcast. It became a signal beam that struck the huddled gannets, turned off suddenly, its light deflected, the sun still concealed.

Abruptly, as though there never had been a dawn, a blue sky or a mortal at the bottom of the cliffs, everything was blotted out in a second squall.

I ran back across the island, through a forest roaring with rain.

The children of a lonely village, cut off from all road and rail communication with the rest of the world, look down at their home.

Norman Dollamount: Sixty thousand miles of rowing.

The scene from Witless Bay: Gull Island in the foreground and Green Island and Great Island in the distance.

At left, the silver light of Bonaventure Island and an old house.

Below, Henry Yard and the author fish breakfast at Witless Bay.

*Gannets in flight
seem to "fly on rails."*

*Sun bursts through overcast at Bonaventure and reveals the
narrow cliff-top colony of the gannets.*

Perce Sturge

Uncle Benny Sturge

Ig Sturge

Art Sturge

Uncle Jacob Sturge

Arold Sturge

Jim Walsh

SOME FACES OF THE PEOPLE OF THE ISLANDS

Jim Walsh's children

Gulls at Kent Island and a bird who stood in a tree and said "Gome."

Female gull, attacking in defense of her nest.

*Two gull chicks stand
at the edge of an abyss.*

At left, gannets surrounded by a sea of murres on Funk Island. Above, murre about to smash into teeming masses beneath. Below, Gull Island at night, with author and petrel caught together for one unreal second by the camera.

Puffins sweep across
Great Island at dusk.

Commander of the
puffins. His lieutenants
await his orders.

9

Incident at Cape St. Mary's

THE DAY BEGAN at three thirty, as I stood in heavy rain and drank a bottle of New-foundland beer. I had not eaten breakfast and the beer did not go down well. But it triggered events which took me to the barrens and to an unmarked grave.

For more than a week, poised at the edge of Witless Bay, I had waited for one clear dawn which would give me a fine day to see and photograph the birds of the islands. But day followed day with chill mist, rain, and high winds. A heavy overcast cloaked the coast. Northern summers are unpredictable as death, and if you ask a native whether tomorrow will be fine, he looks at you, astonished. How could anyone know tomorrow's weather?

One afternoon early, the sky cleared in an hour and I headed for Witless Bay. As I left the bitumen road and roared along gravel, the air lightened. My spirits lifted; I rounded a bend, topped a hill, and skidded to a stop. Mist straddled the road like a high wall. I drove through it, but I knew I was beaten. Dispirited, I returned to St. John's. There must be a demon of Witless

Bay, I thought, who frustrated travelers with thin
pocketbooks and short tempers.

The bad weather persisted. I decided on a flank
attack. Instead of waiting for the day to clear, I would
rise each morning before dawn and be at Witless Bay
in time for sunrise, if it came. The next morning, I got
up at three, looked into a black and glittering sky, and
drove south at high speed. I was so absorbed by the
thought of a clear sky and dawn that I scarcely noticed
the first drops of rain on the windshield. I stopped,
looked out the window. No stars. The air breathed with
that soft sound which mist seems to make. I drove on,
determined to cast off the burden of my frustration.
Finally, a faint light showed in the heavy rain and I
stopped beyond the crest of a hill. Wet silence extended
out to sea. I had never seen such a negative, hopeless
sight.

In the half-light, a pair of headlights stalked me in
the rear-vision mirror. A pick-up truck crunched to a
halt beside me and a mad face peered out of the driver's
window. We looked at each other and then, impatient,
he gestured to me to wind down my window.

"Washa . . . washa . . . washa . . ."

His mouth was full of nails.

"Washa . . . washa . . . DOANG?"

The last word burst out in a cloud of spittle. When
I got out of my car and went to his window, I realized
the cab of the truck contained three of the worst drunks
I had ever seen. They moved and spoke in ridiculous

slow motion.

"Washa . . . washa . . . washa . . . ?"

I was waiting to go out to the island.

"Aaaaaaar!"

The men were delighted. A hand fumbled in a box and brought out a bottle of beer. The cap was nipped off and I was handed a foaming bottle.

"Drink . . . drink . . . drink . . . UP!"

The drink bridged the gulf between them and my own sobriety. But our language problem was impossible. They looked waveringly at me, eyes crisscrossed, wanting to communicate but unable to articulate the words. I downed another bottle and with great formality we shook hands and the truck edged off down the hill at two miles an hour.

The cold beer swilled in my empty stomach and gave my frustration a touch of hysteria. Why should this day be wasted? I might as well go *somewhere*. I felt the need to travel. Because island-hunting was impossible, I decided on another expedition and remembered there was a big bird colony about a hundred and fifty miles away, on a lonely part of the southern shore. There, in the days when ornithologists still collected birds' eggs, a man named John Cahoon made himself briefly famous by climbing alone to reach the nests of the solan goose, or gannet, as the bird is called now. He had fallen and died on the rocks. The story of Cahoon and his lonely climb had always fascinated me. He had climbed at the edge of the barrens: wild, untreed, peatlands which, in the words of one writer, "are so ugly they would break your pen to write about them." Big cliffs, barren lands, rain, a lonely death; they would match this day. I turned the car around and headed for Cape St. Mary's.

The roads were dreadful, a foot under water in some places. The rain was glutinous on the windshield. I hissed past dejected cottages at the edge of scummy brown lakes, through rolling hills dark green with scrub, and never once saw a man, or a car, until I reached the coast. Then, the world changed sharply.

I was at Placentia. The spectacular coastline jutted somberly out of sight; the empty eyes of wartime fortifications squinted across the bay. Hollow concrete structures suggested archaeological ruins rather than recent works of man. Churchill and Roosevelt met here in 1941; men stood in these forts and watched the *Augusta* and the *Prince of Wales* anchored together. Now, rain dripped down concrete into green mold and rubbish.

This coast of Newfoundland has a marvelous, unfettered freedom which exposes the traveler to sweeping views of dark rock, tumbled grass, spruce, and white-rimmed waves. Hundreds of wheeling sea birds speck the sky.

The road dipped into valley after valley. At the bottom of each was a tiny, silent hamlet, every one the same, though the farther south I drove, the deeper into the ground each hamlet seemed to settle. During the thirty-mile drive down the coast, I saw no one.

The road ended at St. Bride's, and I asked a man for directions. Like a Londoner, no Newfoundlander ever admits he cannot direct a traveler. He gives instructions of such demonic concept that the traveler is led mercilessly down side roads; his car bogs in swamps or lumber-camp sawdust; he finds himself on private roads where armed men berate him for trespassing. I discovered that left usually meant right, a few hundred yards invariably meant ten miles, and straight ahead meant anything you might imagine. St. Bride's is the finest direction-giving town in Newfoundland, and its people could pass as Londoners any day.

I had driven there knowing that I must walk thirteen miles to Cape St. Mary's, across the barrenlands.

"Oh no, sir!" the man said. "The road goes all the way now to Cape St. Mary's."

I followed his directions and ended up in the backyard of a house.

"Yes," the woman said, "the road *is* through, but you must go east a couple of miles, then turn south."

I followed these directions and found myself in a gravel pit. Men mending the road said, "No, not here. Back at St. Bride's, that's where the road goes to St. Mary's."

Back at St. Bride's, a fish-plant processor said, "No, no the road isn't through. There's only a track. But man, you'll never make it today. You'll be sucked down in the bog like an animal."

I looked at the map and decided I would drive as close as possible to Cape St. Mary's, then try to make it on foot.

I left St. Bride's and set out east across the true barrens, my first meeting with them. The impact seemed to slow the car, entangling and clotting its vital gears. I yielded and stopped. Nothing moved. I stood at the edge of the road and looked out over endless green tundra. No sound. The wet road wound into a bank of mist clutching a distant hill. The empty deadness of the road suggested that no car had ever traveled it. When a car *did* appear, it passed swiftly and the driver did not look at me. In the silence that followed, I felt a pull from the barrens, like the hypnotic impulse to fall from a high place.

The turnoff road was not marked. An ancient signpost rotting in peat revealed nothing except a vivid obscenity scratched on it with a nail. I turned down the road anyway and headed south toward Point Lance. By now, it was raining gently, and when Point Lance came into view, it was washed in green moisture, its main street a glistening tongue of water. A sleek survey ship lay anchored in the bay. Nothing moved on it: no sign of life on the bridge, boat deck, aft, or forrard.

I drove down into the village and pushed through sheets of water which curled away and lapped at the walls of houses. A hundred windows questioned my presence. But no shade twitched; no blind moved; no human eye peered through a crack. I was a Vandal riding into ruined Amiens, a man of the *Afrika Korps* tanking into Bengasi. I tipped into a declivity as a yellow wave rose up the hood, and the silent village dropped behind.

The road, which I was now bound to pursue to its end, rose along an incision cut out of coastal cliffs. It was no longer graveled; the surface was bare clay, sleek as wet silk. I climbed, and the car slipped toward the edge of the cliff, where gray water moved among strewn rocks. Rain pelted down. Gusts of wind shook the car. The car slid. I knew, with certainty, that the wreckage of a New York automobile, arctic water washing through its broken windows, would arouse no attention in this place.

I rounded a corner by driving crabwise. The right headlight gouged the soft earth from the cliff and the tail of the car swung over the edge. I could have predicted the road's end: a collection of lifeless shanties with not one footprint in the muddy road to remind me I was among men.

My path to Cape St. Mary's led to my right, up steep hills covered with clustered masses of scrub spruce and fir and only traversable by the bed of a muddy stream. If the coast was all like this, the Cape St. Mary's trip would be impossible.

There was another problem. Though I did not believe any vehicle had ever traveled this road, I still could not leave my car blocking its single lane. But when I pulled off the road and got out, the car began to slip sideways. I braced myself against the roof gutter for a moment, in a strain of muscle, then leaped inside and gunned the car back on to the road. Eventually, I found a stony shoulder, not too close to the cliff, and balanced the car there.

The wind was now almost a gale. The survey ship's stern pointed at me as I faced east. With the wind came mist that swept across the bay in uncanny compact masses, one moment obscuring the ship, the next instant touching my eyes, then whisking up the side of the hill in silent flight.

By this time, I was dismayed by the hostile surroundings. I turned with relief toward a man who appeared on the road from the village. He was tall and lean, dressed like a fisherman in stout boots, nondescript, loose-fitting pants, leather jacket and cap. He carried a small food pack slung over his shoulder. He walked with a solid, swinging stride which took him squarely between my wheel tracks. I moved around the back of the car to intercept him.

He came on, eyes directed straight ahead. Weakly, I gestured a salute. His automaton eyes did not flicker. I held my ground. At ten paces, I gestured again, and opened my mouth to shout a greeting above the wind. But his eyes never shifted. He came on, passed me with twelve inches separating our shoulders, and was gone into the rain.

I had seen a dead man from that dead village; he was bound for that cluster of dead shanties at the end of the road. The earth suppurated. Bubbles burst in rotting turf. Streams of gray liquid spilled over grass.

I confronted two selves. One was a seventeen-year-old youth, lean as whipcord and hard as steel, who went up the sides of mountains like a goat. The other was a thirty-six-year-old expatriate, similar in appearance, but soft as a ripe peach from years of pushing pens instead of swinging axes, all his power stuffed inside his fat head.

The hill disappeared in the running mist. Beyond it lay other hills, ravines: wetness and cold and slippery slopes. There was the possibility of a broken leg. Alone on those barrens? The imagination, useful for writing, makes a poor hero. Yet there was an inevitability about this trip. I was not really surprised to find the pack on my back, with the camera wrapped in waterproof plastic. The long climb up the wet hill began.

At the top of the hill came a charge of adrenalin that transformed the day and the place. Stretched before me was an expanse of hills, smooth and seductive. They flowed across my sight to vertical cliffs which walked along the coast and disappeared. I stood there, caught by the grand scheme of the earth's design. The wind tugged at my pack; behind, a tiny car by a ribbon of mud, a silent toy ship in a bay; ahead, a land created by imagination. I felt a magnetic pull to walk freely in those green hills.

I walked for an hour, down from the hill, down through swampy valleys, down through scattered patches of spruce, up into ridged hills, then I began to understand the scope and depth of the land. I walked another hour, an ant working across a football field.

Despite rain and mist, I saw the configuration of the coastline. In front of me was a large bay ending in a headland. Beyond that was another headland, perhaps seven miles away. Beyond that, I knew, was Cape St. Mary's and its gannets.

The bay was alive and brilliant with gannets—about two thousand were collected on the water. Some birds dived sporadically into the shallows with easy, fluid grace, tiny players on a huge stage. I trudged west and watched them diving for capelin which were prowling the coastline in search of beaches on which to spawn.

I considered trying to photograph the birds, but mist rolled across the bay, scarcely fifty feet high, dense as detergent foam. It overwhelmed the gannets. Some of them flew above it and circled high. Others broke through it and appeared dimly, almost at my feet, the mist clinging to them until they flew free. The mist darkened and my view of the bay was blotted out.

I walked for two hours. I slid down steep ravines, climbed vertical banks, and experienced the nemesis of the soft man in the outdoors: I was tiring faster than I was keeping warm. The cold, abetted by the gale, was stiffening my fingers and I had trouble fumbling the straps of my pack into position. The wind was so bad in places I had to crawl to avoid being blown down. The rain increased, reduced my vision to near zero. Several times narrow slits opened in front of me and I looked two hundred feet down to white water moving soundlessly on the rocks. I was caught in hurricane blasts of wind, funneled and compressed in the cliffs. One gust hurled me down a long slope. My brain was numb and I could hardly think of another four or five miles of this, and then the return.

Perhaps it was exhaustion, perhaps it was not, but at the height of the wind, a wailing cry asked my attention. It was neither angry nor menacing, simply imploring. If it was an animal sound, it managed to suggest a human quality.

"I am lost," it said clearly. "Help me."

I listened, but I heard nothing more except the sough of wind at the cliff edge and the hiss of distant waves. I turned toward the cliff and at once I saw the cross. It was driven into the sod about a foot from the edge of the cliff, weathered silver. It made no sense for anyone to be buried in such a place, yet it could scarcely be a practical joke. The cross was undeniably *there*, and the grass humped slightly away from it. A grave?

The question brought an answer. The rain stopped; the mist lifted abruptly, and I saw that any man who knew this bay might want to stay here; headlands cut dark patterns and they enclosed cliffs, rock slides, tiny beaches, white-fringed reefs. The cross stood black against an incandescent sea; light spilled from holes ripped in the overcast. For a second I saw the sun, a chunk bitten out of it, and remembered it was the day of an eclipse.

I looked beyond the cross. The gannets had come close inshore and were diving steadily. They glided by me at eye level and then fell away toward the water. Every muscle action was visible in detail. I dived with the gannets, looked over their shoulders as they turned away and fell. It was not an abandoned free fall, as it appeared to be. Each dive was a series of tricky adjustments, made at better than a hundred miles an hour, to keep the bird aimed at a target not more than a few inches square. The diving birds' tails twisted slightly; the wings adjusted infinitesimally as they counteracted wind drift and turbulence by sharpening or flattening the fall. It was deliberate and knowing, perfection to watch. It reminded me of the submarine murres, the bird metropolises, the burrowing sea birds, the suggestion of how the rigors of environment could be overcome.

The free fall of the gannets seemed suicidal. How could this conglomerate of thrust-out wings and body hit the water at such speed and survive? The birds dived with six-foot wings slightly crooked to stabilize the flying machine, but at the last second hinged them straight back from the shoulder sockets and folded them against their bodies. They hit the water slim and straight as missiles.

I have digressed; I did not spend hours watching the birds. It was an explosion of sensation, over in a few minutes. As I watched, I reached for the telescopic camera, which would see the blink of a gannet's eyelid as it hit the water. I reached, but my hand disobeyed

me and remained clawed. I instructed the other hand
to grip the camera. But it was equally numb. I lifted the
camera between my wrists, but I could not get a forefinger to the shutter release or move the lens to focus.
The gannets rose and fell, so close I could hear them
striking the sea like downflung boomerangs.

No disappointment ahead could equal those moments. I crouched on the wet ground and the gannets
passed me, silent ships of flight, dark eyes appraising me.
They turned, adjusted, fell away, adjusted, adjusted,
and disappeared in columns of water. Frozen as my
hands were, a warm flush crept up my back. I looked at
the gannets and sought to know them. But they wheeled
away wildly and the fish were driven deeper; the gannets moved offshore.

The moment had arrived to make a crucial decision:
go on and gamble that I could make it back, or be pru-
dent and assume that the nearby headland (two miles
away?) did not conceal Cape St. Mary's at all. As I huddled in the lea of a rock, munching cold meat, the decision was made for me. The wind rose sharply. The
sea and shore disappeared in a blanket of rain. Water
seethed down the steep slopes of the ravine. A stream
at the bottom swelled visibly. I was beaten. I turned
east and pushed, like an old man, against that hellish
wind.

The Cape St. Mary's trip was a failure, but there was
an epilogue. The day was now fifteen hours old and had
encompassed one hundred miles of driving, prebreak-

fast drinking, twenty miles of walking, an eclipse of the sun, exhaustion and exposure, and a skin-tingling spell of bird watching, and it was not yet finished.

The epilogue was waiting at a gas station on the way back to St. John's. I was preoccupied and the gas gauge had gone to empty. Service stations in Newfoundland occur haphazardly and give a special zest to driving. The gas-station attendant may serve you, but then he may not. He may be away fishing, or hunting moose; or he may be asleep.

When *this* gas station loomed up, I doubted that I could rouse any one at such a deserted-looking and ramshackle place. The last gallon of gas had been hand-pumped, it seemed, into a glass-curtained Franklin tourer round 1926. The rusted station sign dated from the twenties.

The shanties beyond the pumps slumbered in pale rain. I walked to the nearest shanty and pushed the door. Inside, it was dark as a cave and until my eyes adjusted to the gloom, I thought the place was empty. But then, tingling, I saw the dark room filled with silent people. There must have been sixty of them—small children, young men, women, oldsters—leaning against walls and counters, sitting on boxes or on the floor. I could tell by their expressions that I was a Martian and they, the Earthlings. They waited for my move.

"Any chance of some gas?"

I was so well accustomed to the Newfoundland temperament that I knew there would be no answer. A solemn eight-year-old sucked his thumb. Long silence. What was there to say? The crowd relaxed a little. It found me interesting. It would watch me just as long as I stood there.

A tall, cadaverous man stepped out of the crowd and shuffled toward me. At a distance of fifteen inches, he drew in a big breath, and addressed a shattering bellow at point-blank range. It was Uncle Benny again, but much louder and (I could hardly believe this) more incomprehensible. Not one intelligible word emerged from the roaring noise.

"Oh, ah, yes," I said.

He clapped me on the back and the bellows resumed. I grinned weakly at the silent figures in the background. But they were unsympathetic. The bellows ended on a note of interrogation and I responded.

"I've been down to Cape St. Mary's."

A great roar of delight followed, and in the ensuing jumble of speech, one word emerged, like a bluebell in a blizzard.

Cahoon!

The mention of the stricken egg collector was the introduction to a sustained narrative that had intensity, conviction, and excitement. The narrator's body tensed and swayed, his big hands cut the air as he threw imaginary ropes up cliff faces, and within minutes, I was with him in his story, carried along by the clarity of his gestures.

He clawed for a handhold and his booted feet kicked

against a rock. I found myself with my face pressed against the rock face, looking down at the sea. Above was the nest of a solan goose and another egg for the ornithologist William Brewster. The rope flapped against the rock and I felt my aloneness. What if I fell? Well, no matter. Nothing could be done about it, anyway. This work had to be finished.

All during the climb the rotten rock had given me trouble. This cliff face was no different. I reached for a new hold, my foot broke off a large chunk of rock, and I was falling! A scream in the throat, rocks rushing up, whitened bone on rock, crushed oblivion; I was dead. The sea washed my feet.

The roaring stopped. The storyteller was done. Sixty silent people looked at me. The cadaverous man clapped me on the shoulder again and shuffled back to a half-empty bottle of Coke standing on a window ledge.

A small brown man, who looked like a bird, was at my elbow.

"Oi filled your tank, sor, and that will be noine dollars and fower cents."

10

At Witless Bay

BEFORE DEPARTING for an island, the traveler is uncomfortably split. He seeks to change his status, leave the mainland, and become, however briefly, an islander. This, in concert with the invariable uncertainty of the journey, leaves him dubious. If he does reach the island, he has lost his freedom to leave at will. He is a civilized man on the mainland; once away from it, he may reveal another side of himself.

I stood on a hill at Witless Bay and looked down at thin bands of mist moving inshore; a hint of rain was in the air. It had been raining for ten days, stormy for fourteen. Offshore lay Gull Island which, even after I had experienced islands of manifold moods, still remained the most seductive with its promise of a mystery revealed, the nocturnal invasion of petrels.

Yet, watching, I had to admit my conceit. Gull Island was built of my imagination. This lump of soulless earth had no meaning except to a handful of fishermen who used it as an anchorage in time of storm, and a few ornithologists interested in sea birds. My rage to reach it came not from the light side of nature, but from a possessive urge to illuminate it selfishly, to be the first man to see it truly. I could not merely see and remember it. I had to write about it.

There was something else; for some days, I had felt growing irritation. I was petulant, a middle-aged farceur. The journey was more than half over. I had been successful, skillful even, in traveling. But memory had become an impediment. The youth of the journey was vivid, the ironic clarity of impression of a comity of gulls at work, the simple stillness of a sleeping island, the vision of death in a colony of murres.

Now, however, each step I took was more difficult than the last, which was not what I had envisaged earlier in the journey. Each day brought a growing sense of futility. I had set out in search of insight, yet my experiences were forming themselves into an inexorable pattern which, I knew, must have a final act. But what ending might I seek? I sensed it lay on Gull Island and my failure to reach the island added to the feeling of futility. Worst thought of all: if Gull Island proved elusive, perhaps the rest of the summer was ephemera, too.

A cap of mist formed on Gull Island and confused its shape. As I drove down into the valley of Witless Bay, the island disappeared behind the mist. Before dark, heavy rain fell and the wind rose sharply.

Before dawn the next morning, I walked down a grassy track winding among sleeping houses. Bill White, a local fisherman, walked ahead of me toward the basin where the boat was moored. As we clumped downhill, we met Henry Yard, a shy, taciturn fisherman who was the other boatman. How was it?

"It doesn't look good," he said.

I expected this. If I could not land this day, I might never reach the island. The weather forecast was for high winds and rain. That might mean the end of summer and the end of the journey, right here on this ramshackle jetty, standing shivering in the dark. I scraped shin and elbow climbing over the high sides of the dory, but now had no feeling of objective which would make the journey reasonable.

We were the first boat out of Witless Bay and the heavy thud-thud-thud of the single-cylinder engine lashed back at us from the shore. We hit the first oceanic waves. The heavy boat rose steeply and fell. I was in the bows and felt I was going to the bottom of the sea, or to hell. The bows slammed down and the impact sent white spume fleeing on either side of me. The boat rose again and stars, moon, and stomach wheeled crazily. Once, flying in a storm in a clipper ship, I had been the only passenger who had taken lunch, and I wondered what had happened to that stomach of twenty years ago.

I wore two undershirts, a thick workshirt, a cashmere pullover, a nylon jacket, a sheep's-wool longshoreman's jacket, but I was cold. Yard and White, motionless and stoic in the stern, dripped water from their oilskins. The eastern sky lightened behind Gull Island, and looking at it, I recalled my warm sleeping bag, sensuous comfort, solicitude, blue waves curling in the sun, and wondered what in the hell had brought me here. I wanted to be home, wherever that was. The wind rushed, like a swollen aerial river, in the spruces of imagination, and petrels cried across the bare chill wastes of another planet, where a man died after he had heard their voices.

The red rim of the sun appeared at the edge of a jagged cloud and was absolutely heatless. Could this be the same sun that had struck me at Bonaventure? Of course it was not. That had been a young sun; this one was pallid with age. Gull Island darkened in shadow and we pitched along its northern shore. I looked at White, and he shook his head. No landing today. We rounded the island and turned south. White knew my feelings. He crawled forward and bawled over the engine:

"A couple of fellers lived there for a while. They were strangers from the far-off parts. They dug the biggest hole you ever saw. You could put a house in it, I would say."

He gestured at the island, now tinted faintly orange, and I saw the scar of man's digging, a raw mark spanning a gully and flanked by the blobs of gulls.

"When they came off the island, I never saw two men so marvelously thinned down. People said they were looking for treasure buried by some of them fellers in the pirate days."

As we plunged on, an oppressive vision came of the men who had preceded me to the islands: auk hunters and their slaughter which earned a dollar and wiped out a million years of evolution; the ruins of Hay Island and the triumph of the ducks; the overgrown fields of Bonaventure; the insane treasure hunters who could believe a buccaneer would sail two thousand miles to bury booty. Man had appeared on the islands, a flicker in the eyelid of time, and had been thrown out. Now came the observer, and he was sluggish under the weight of his history.

We were heading directly into a swell and the movement of the boat was viciously accentuated. One mile ahead Green Island jutted out of the sea. I had no interest in it now, but Henry Yard, at the tiller, had decided he would let me see it in circumnavigation. It was even more unattainable than Gull Island because landings on it are possible only in pacific weather. But as we approached, it imposed itself on us. It rose very tall, no longer an island, but a Wagnerian crescendo. The vertical sides were tiered with birds. Every foothold, every ledge, every cranny more than an inch wide, was occupied. The sound of the engine cannonaded against the stone walls; a cloud of puffins blossomed; kittiwakes swept away from the cliffs.

Go-away, go-away, go-away!

The moat of the sea rose cleanly up the walls, fell back into itself with a silent splash of white. A stream of murres poured out of a canyon and shot, crossbow bolts, overhead. Despite my torpor, I felt stirred.

White shouted, "How about that!"

We were performers in the amphitheater, and the stadium spectators roared and milled. Streams of birds spilled off cliff tops and the bright, surprised faces of puffins looked down on us as they hovered, facing into the wind, seeking to appraise our intent.

We rounded the southern end of the island and the wind threw us a gush of sound, so loud it diminished the hammering of the engine. It leaped out of an incision in the rock into which was packed a black seething mass of murres. Their voices were concentrated in the restricted space and mingled with our noise, the sounds ricocheted with mechanistic energy.

"Did you ever see anything like *that!*"

The murres came at us in an avalanche of life that dropped away from the walls of the incision, coalesced, and spilled into our wide eyes. Then slowly, like the sound of a siren fading on a turnpike, the roar from the incision diminished, and we were left looking backward at the cornucopia endlessly spilling its creatures into the air. White and Yard were grinning. Now, that was worth seeing!

Midway along the western shore, now in shadow, and seeing the sun, in full brilliance, bursting around the colonnades of the island, Henry Yard cut the engine and we drifted, wallowing. All right; that's enough. Now, let's go home. Henry Yard jerked me out of it.

"Give Mr. Russell a jig."

I found myself lowering the jig into the water without fully comprehending what I was doing. I knew that cod-jigging was an archaic method of catching fish, developed thousands of years ago when primitive man discovered that at certain times the cod is so voracious it will strike at almost anything. The jig is a lead weight, crudely shaped to resemble a small fish. Fastened to it are two or three substantial hooks.

The jig is lowered into the water among feeding cod, and after a moment, it is jerked upward sharply. Any cod interested in the jig will, according to the theory, be snagged by its sharp uprising. In my nauseated, negative frame of mind, this seemed pointless.

"Well," White said, seeing my face, "we might as well fish, now we're out here."

I felt the weight hit bottom and drew the line up slightly. Then, holding the line firmly over my right forefinger, I drew the line up swiftly about two feet, let it fall back, drew it up sharply again. On the second pull, the line caught on something and tautened.

"He's got one," White said. He was pulling a fish up himself.

I did not feel the thrill a fisherman might experience seeing his fly or spoon sucked down. I did feel disbelief. How could such a moronically simple device trap an oceanic fish? There was no cod down there.

But as I drew the line up, it resisted with strong jerks. I was not prepared, however, for the huge fish which came lashing into sight. I yanked it over the gunwale and thirty pounds of codfish flopped down. I was hypnotized. Ridiculous! Down went the jig, and this time one pull on the line brought the heaviness, the struggle, the frantic, hand-over-hand pull on the line. The fish wrenched out of the water. I caught a third fish, a fourth, a fifth; it was unbelievable. I noticed blood streaming down my hands as I pulled up the sixth and seventh fishes, but I felt no pain.

I was a primitive, a savage, unheeding: No trace of nausea now. Not a shiver in my body; instead, a hot, exultant sweat. The cries from Green Island no longer were the lost voices of animals, crying from their repellent home. Now, they were friendly and beckoning. I knew them again. As I caught the fish, I knew I would return to these islands and conquer them. Nothing mattered except this moment where, in an unspeakable part of the psyche, the act of killing was the sole reason for existence. The fish came up endlessly; two hundred, three hundred, four hundred pounds. I lost all sense of reality as the pile grew around my feet.

Dimly, I was aware of the other two men and the rhythm of their jigging, which was as fruitful as mine: grunts, flappings, the slap of line against wet oilskin, the jagged tear of hooks wrenched out of mouths, the floppings of stricken fish.

My jig caught fish under bottom jaws, hooked their gills, ripped their bellies, snagged their tails. They came up through the green water backward, sideways, forward, struggling, inert. I slipped and fell on fish, kicked them aside, I felt them slither around my ankles, rise to my calves. I had a fleeting, bizarre thought that we might go on catching cod until the boat sank under us.

Far back in my mind came a dim picture of men I had seen behaving as I was now behaving. Several hundred wild goats were driven against a cliff, and men, some of them my friends, directed rifle fire among the animals, who bleated, reared, bellowed, bled, and fell. The men fired, eyes bright, oblivious, jaws knotting, in silent, terrible concentration. I saw a shark come into the shallows and two friends go after it with knives; again that terrifying concentration of the man-killer as knives rose and fell.

Then, as suddenly as it had begun, the jigging was over.

"They're gone," Henry Yard said.

It was a door closing, a friendship breaking. In a brief, murderous hour I had been rejuvenated. My hands were bloody and caked with slime; the right palm was blistered and ripped, a ghoul's hand from the make-up department. The arctic wind was cold steel on my wet forehead. My eyes smarted with salt.

Slowly, I brought myself back from the hunting frenzy. Henry Yard moved methodically around the cramped area of the punt's stern. He dug out an armful of wood from a locker under the stern counter, laid it crisscrossed on a metal plate, splashed it with some gasoline, and set it on fire. He had already peeled potatoes and laid pieces of pork in a cast-iron frypan.

Then he rummaged at his feet and held up a small, well-formed cod weighing about eight pounds. While the pork fat hissed and crackled, he handed the fish to Bill White. Both men examined it. White hefted it, nodded, and took out his knife.

As he did, a knot of hunger tightened in my stomach. I looked inward and asked, astonished, *Is this the same man who watched the dawn behind Gull Island? Where is the shivering coward of an hour ago?* The smell of fat frying in the arctic air and the prospect of eating fresh fish filled me with the greatest feeling of well-being I have ever had.

Bill White's knife went into the belly of the fish, ripped downward, and the guts flopped and hung.

"Now," he said with relish, "the best parts of the cod usually go to waste because people don't know about them. But there's some real delicacies here."

His knife slid into the cod and he isolated an organ with his fingers. He cut it free, then smoothed it out on a hatch cover. It was the cod's stomach. He ran his knife across its surface, cutting into rows of nodules to prevent the organ from curling.

"This is great when you fry it," he said.

In went the knife again. An uproar on Green Island sent birds mushrooming over it. White waited for quiet.

"Now this," he said, holding a tiny red organ between thumb and forefinger, "this is the greatest delicacy of all. The heart. Some people have the patience to take the hearts out of a hundred fish to make a small meal. I've seen fellers at fish plants digging them out of cod and eating them raw, with blood running down their faces."

He used the knife again and out came a reddish mass of globules, about six inches long.

"Some people like this," he said. "The roe. But I don't eat it."

He tossed it over the side. Overboard with the roe went the long pink mass of the cod liver, which is prized by deep-sea gourmets when grilled over a birch-wood fire, dunked in salt water, and eaten scalding hot. I asked him about the liver, but White dismissed it.

"Too rich."

With the cod cleaned, he split the fish, then ran his knife along the backbone, isolating a narrow strip of white gristle.

"This is what we call the sound," he said. "Delicious, but you need a hundred to make a meal."

It went over the side. He beheaded the fish, and I knew what was coming next.

"You've eaten cod tongues?" Yes, I had.

It has always puzzled me that cod tongues are not a favorite epicurean item. They can stand comparison with caviar, filet mignon, truffles. Perhaps they travel poorly, or must be ocean-fresh, otherwise they would be better known. No matter. *I* have had them.

White ran his knife around the inside of the bottom jawbone and plucked out the thick mass of gristle and white flesh. It is called the tongue, but it is nothing of the sort. He was about to throw it away when I caught his hand.

"I'll cook it," I said.

He flung the head overboard. At least two more

delicacies, the cod's cheeks and the head itself, had gone into the water.

In the meantime, Henry Yard had chopped the cod into chunks. He piled cut-up potatoes, onions, cod pieces, and lumps of fried salt pork into a large cast-iron pot and added fresh water from a bottle. He put the pot on the wood fire.

I looked at that pot with every memory of every campfire, every boyhood experience in the woods, clear in my mind. This was antelope grilling on a spit, a twenty-pound rainbow trout steaming on hot coals. The pot exuded heady, intoxicating odors. Surely the gods ate ambrosia only because they knew nothing about cod cooked in a Newfoundland punt.

While we waited for the main course to cook, I fried the cod tongue in salt-pork fat. It needed only a moment, just enough to heat it and sear the outer layer of tissue. The result was a rich globule of pure-white flesh, lightly browned on the outside. By the time I had eaten it, the smell from the big pot was unbearable.

"Let's eat," Bill White said, finally.

Henry Yard served. He spooned out chunks of fish dripping with fragrant liquid which permeated the potatoes. Conversation ceased. The only sounds were the screams and yells from Green Island. We emptied our plates, crammed big chunks of thickly buttered, home-made bread into our mouths. The plates were filled and emptied again before talk was possible.

"Funny thing," Bill White said. "The cod has a different taste out here on the water. It don't ever taste the same on land."

I lay in the bows, cold white sun in my eyes. Green Island released showers of birds who twisted overhead on their way to hunt nearby in shallow water, the fertile sea highlands where fish came to graze. We—fishermen, birds, fish—were all here for different reasons yet, in the end, for the same reason. Bill White stood over me, anchor rope in hand.

"You'll get wet"

Who cared? The boat trembled and rattled and Green Island turned away from the sun. Bill White sat down and told about Witless Bay. In late June, capelin (herringlike fish) appeared, millions strong, and sought shelving beaches to spawn on. In the early summer, countless launce, small, eel-like fish, appeared in the bay and boiled to the surface. In August, pothead whales prowled the bay, probably in pursuit of squid who, in turn, were pursuing the capelin or the launce that had preceded them. Schools of tuna roamed across the bay. Finally, in winter, long after the petrels and kittiwakes, the puffins and the murres, had deserted the two islands, thousands of eider ducks arrived to dive to the beds of shellfish which lay sixty feet beneath our keel as we sailed now.

Set against this aloof and constant regeneration of life, age became unimportant and the seasons had no special significance except as impartial segments of time; even that might not be important.

By the time we arrived at the boat mooring, I was nearly asleep, warm and satisfied. I helped haul the dory up the slipway, but it was the effort of a somnambulist. The houses of Witless Bay flashed windows at us. I felt like a man who knew all the seasons and lived equally in each. It must be late afternoon, I thought. I looked at my watch.

It was seven thirty in the morning.

11

The Men of the Islands

MIDWAY IN THE SUMMER, a fisherman was rowing me across a small harbor enclosed by steep slopes which held water black as ebony. Amber squares glowed in terraced lines above me from the night-burning lamps of the fishing village we were leaving. He stopped rowing and we drifted.

"It's a pretty sight, isn't it, sir?" he said.

I noticed a band of violet forming above the topmost houses. It would soon be dawn. The amber squares dulled. Yes, very pretty.

"It's a funny thing," he said. "When I were young, I never saw them lights. *Now*, I see them. I *remember* them when I am out on the water. Now, sir, what do you make of that?"

The men of the islands live in a suspension of time, in a microclimate, a scientist might say, in which the physical presence of reality is at their elbow at all times. They play no harpsichords, read no Caesar, though they would understand Vercingetorix very well. They are concerned only with the skeleton of living. Outwardly, at least, it is the bone and not the brain which is abraded. Uncle Sam may go insane, Cousin Edward may be born a cripple, and that is the way of things.

The real issues are arrivals, departures, tides, warmth, cold, and death. I helped a fisherman push his keel into deeper water; he sniffed the sea air, remembering a wreck on a shoal and the bodies of two friends on a beach. Once, he had gone through a year when he caught nothing and his family nearly starved. He expected this and knew how to deal with it.

"A hard time," he said with a smile.

No bitterness.

"If I had my time again," said Jim Walsh, a fisherman from southeastern Newfoundland, "I might not go to sea. But I don't regret what I have done."

In his worst year, Walsh housed and fed his family on four hundred dollars.

The men of the islands maintain their enduring dignity. They are steadfast and happy regardless of whether they are friendly or unfriendly, and they can be either. A visitor in their homes can only feel disquiet at the subversion of the spirit in city slums, where human beings, far better off, far more sophisticated, cannot cope with life.

I landed, a stranger, on an island, and within fifteen minutes was sitting down to a three-course meal of moose, smoked salmon, and bakeapples, served me by two people I did not know. One islander, hearing a rumor that I was coming to *his* island, met every boat from the mainland for two weeks, until he triumphantly marched up the gangplank to welcome me.

Island men do not regard time as we do. Time, on an island, has a detached quality which makes it meaningless. Today is today. But what is tomorrow? An extension of today? A part of next year? Never?

The contradiction of time unmasked me. Why did I feel compelled to reach this island, that island? Only because of the urgency and the belief I had brought with me, and these, I knew from the islanders, had no significance. My frustration amused them.

"Next summer," they said, comfortingly, as we leaned into an Atlantic gale, not able to reach an island.

I waited on the banks of a tickle for a mailboat to take me to an island. I waited a day, two days. Where was the mailboat? Nobody knew. Perhaps the boatman had forgotten. Let's go and find him. The boatman was in bed.

"Tomorrow, tomorrow," he said.

I was on the point of reaching another island when the fishing boat broke down. Its owner hand-cranked it three thousand times, from six until eleven in the morning. Then we ran aground in a cove. There was a clergyman with me on the boat. He was making his rounds.

"If you lived here," he said, watching me shrewdly, "you would go mad."

It was a bitter truth. I had become forced to doubt myself as the journey persisted. At the start of the summer, I left for each island without much thought of anything except *getting* there. My motives were selfish and withdrawn. But gradually, I was being forced to think like an islander. I looked into the predawn darkness and considered the barriers: not ideas, men, or money, but the physical force of earth—tides, currents, mist, rain, wind, and waves.

This was simple, and it was easy to think that I was dealing with a simple people. But when I put my life against theirs, I suffered by comparison. My exotic tales of far-off places had a strangely banal ring. In response, they showed me what they knew.

I was talking with a group of fishermen, a storekeeper, a plumber, and a handyman on one small island when a man, silent for an hour, leaned forward and said: "I do believe, sir, that you are going to have hard times."

When?

"Soon, sir, very soon, I'm afraid."

The remark meant nothing until much later, when my islands visit was finished and the hard times did, indeed, strike. I struggled to remember that man's face, perform some feat of memory which would explain the inexplicable.

Frequently during the summer, the island men looked, and understood something about me which I did not know myself. I walked into a roomful of people and had the instant and discomfiting sense of being *known* before I said anything.

This was instinctive, I realized, and led back to primitive man. Uncle Benny's extraordinary feats of navigation might be explained as a freakish talent of one man. But islander after islander had that talent. Twice during fifty years of fishing on the banks, a schooner captain, George Follett, returned to his fishing grounds and snagged anchors that he had lost during his previous visit. This would be like walking blindfolded from New York to Boston and picking up a wallet you remembered dropping on a previous walk.

Two fishermen were returning to Witless Bay a few years ago when they were drowned in a squall. Their bodies did not come ashore. The best friend of one of them rowed a mile offshore, dropped a jig into fifteen fathoms, and pulled his friend to the surface.

The traveler finds this metaphysical world cast in classic, repetitive forms. An old woman told me how she awakened one night fifty years ago, got out of bed, and walked to her window. Her husband was standing in oilskins at the end of the porch. She saw him quite clearly and there was no mistaking his identity.

"I knew then," she said, "that there was something wrong."

She had awakened at the time her husband drowned on the Grand Banks and, as she describes it, he hastened home to console his dear wife. He still appears on the porch because, she says, "he knows I am lonely."

Island men feel predestination so clearly they are free to be fearless or foolhardy. They navigate confidently through a black sea bristling with shoals. Uncle Benny, sailing in his paper bag, always knew his time would be long coming. But other islanders are just as positive they will die young. They fall from the decks of longliners and drown instantly; no threshing around or fighting fate. I discussed this with a woman on the south coast, a mainlander married to a Newfoundlander. "It's fantastic how they seem to know," she said. "But it's tragic to see grown and intelligent men so much at the mercy of superstition."

A few years previously, she had been monitoring fishing-boat calls during a storm. Everywhere she turned on the radio dial, "men were dying," but one sinking has stayed in her memory. The skipper of a big fishing boat in difficulties battled the storm for an hour, then gave up.

"What shall I do?" he asked plaintively over the radio. "What shall I do now?"

He was told to hand over command to his first mate. But the mate had given up too.

"No point in trying to do anything," he said calmly. "The men don't think we can come out of this."

The ship sank and the men drowned.

The sea imposes fatalism, but it is not restricted to mariners. I ran through rain from the car to a general store and stumbled into a dim room. In the center sat a short, Buddha-like man. The room was filled, floor to ceiling, with thousands of bottles of beer.

"Come in and have a drink," he said.

He had become rich selling soft drinks and beer, but his material success had not changed his island outlook. His birthplace, a small island two hundred miles away, haunted his heart. A few years before, he had returned there.

"A man can go back to where he was born to, and look down, sir, and practically see his footprints in the earth."

The footprints were no help. He tried people. He remembered the prettiest girl in the village and his friendship with her. But he hardly recognized her; she was fat and frumpish. They relived the old days and recalled almost every heartbeat. She cried. In the end, he left the island depressed and no wiser than before.

He finished his bottle of beer and cracked open a fresh one. He drank all day and every day. I remonstrated with him, but he laughed.

"A man's finished at forty, b'y, finished. There's no point in fighting fate."

The islanders can prove this. Another classic story: Two brothers, one a swimmer, the other not, capsized in a squall while fishing. The nonswimming brother survived, but the swimmer drowned. The islanders say of the survivor, "His time had not come."

The islander may, in his most stubborn incarnation, live alone, determined to see out his life in the place "where he were born to," because that was ordained by fate. I sailed past a cove on an uninhabited coast and saw a solitary house. Who lived *there*?

"Don't go near 'im. 'E be armed and 'e'll shoot anybody who comes close,' my boatman said.

The islander faces the choice of staying at home or of leaving and being totally reincarnated. In one thriving but isolated village, I met a man who had returned to his island. Every morning he left the house in search, as he put it, ". . . of old friends and old times." But each day he returned, baffled and angry. No one remembered him.

"Tomorrow," he would say, with a fresh burst of confidence, "I must try and find . . . now, what was his name . . . ?" The islanders looked at him without sentiment or sympathy. Who was this old fellow? A wheat farmer, did you say?

If he stays at home, the islander preserves his identity, in the manner of an Uncle Benny. When a man on tiny Greenspond Island, on the northeast coast of Newfoundland, was struck down by a ruptured kidney, he had never been off the island in his life and had no desire to leave. But a helicopter picked him up anyway and hustled him south to St. John's, where the kidney was removed. He retained his equanimity at his first experience of airplanes, television, and flush toilets. But as soon as he was well, he demanded to be returned to Greenspond.

"I saw enough," he told me, "to know that there's no future for a man over there. It was rush and bang, shout and stamp, and nobody getting anywhere. Worst of all, they brought me back in an automobile. Now, sir, I can tell you, that is an uncivilized method of travel! No man in his right mind would use it, unless he were insane. I can tell you, sir, without argument, that I will never leave this island again, for any reason. My kidney can give out; my liver can fail; my heart can seize up, but I will never leave this island!"

It rained for three days. The temperature dropped fifty degrees and I was hypnotized in a monotony of running gray skies. I felt the need of company. A helicopter came over some aspens and hovered at my head. A man leaned out and shouted a query. He was lost. Did I know the way to a certain lumber camp? I had seen a sign a few miles back which indicated his direction. Did I feel like a beer? Yes. Follow the helicopter then.

The islanders are beer drinkers. They drink beer with enthusiasm and dedication. Beer is a socializer, a part of the commerce. I sat in the forecastle of a powerful dragger after it had dredged up eighty thousand pounds of codfish from the Grand Banks and discussed with six crew members the differences in their hangovers. They were proud of them. They were self-inflicted; they would disappear. They should be discussed and, as much as possible, enjoyed.

The rain continued and it was Saturday night. Feel like a beer? Yes. Hours later, seven men sat among a hundred and twenty-seven bottles. I watched new-found friends facing each other in owlish contentment. One man fell, going over backward with a crash of bottles, and everybody laughed. Curiously, there was nothing squalid about the scene, but it was clear the islanders found something different from me at the bottom of the bottle.

Their anxiety had a special pressure about it which made me understand their fatalism.

Later, an educated man invited me in out of the rain to discuss the world. There was nothing like living on an island, he said. Occasionally, though, it was interesting to talk to a foreigner. Gave a man perspective. You could not seal yourself entirely off from the world.

But after a few whiskeys, he became morose. These humble islanders were a terrible race of people. They were stupid and ignorant and sometimes quite mad.

"There's no hope for them. Just because they're on an island, they think they can escape the march of progress."

He became steadily more discouraged, and at midnight, after six whiskeys, he got up and went outside. A moment later, I heard a splintering of wood and the ring of breaking glass. From a window, I saw my friend, stripped to the waist, demolishing a small woodshed with an ax. He chopped out the windows and split the door into kindling wood. His wife watched with me.

"Usually," she said calmly, "it's the furniture."

When he came back into the house, he was tired and happy.

"That's better," he said. "Let's have a nightcap."

These people have actual or inherited memory of an age so rigorous that it would kill any modern man. Some survivors still hang on to the old ways. Norman Dollamount, a fisherman of Françoise, a tiny hamlet on Newfoundland's south coast, has rowed sixty thousand miles in fifty years of fishing. He gets up at four o'clock, rows down the long, narrow harbor and out to his fishing grounds. It is an easy row, only two hours out and two hours back. It keeps him independent of gas bills and engine repairs. In winter, he dunks his wool mitts in the water, holds them up until they freeze, and his hands keep nicely warm under the sheath of ice. All that rowing; is it a hardship?

"No, no, sir. It circulates the blood."

Such men were conditioned to the reality of the sea in childhood. Uncle Benny Sturge rode to the Funks when he was four, crammed into the breadbox of his uncle's schooner. Ralph Wright, of Greenspond Island, went to sea at seven, when his father took him along as a cook. On his first trip, the boy was in the galley when a squall overturned the boat. His father and uncle were thrown into the sea, but Wright was trapped inside, buried under dishes and pots. A big wave half righted the boat; water poured into it, and he was swept to freedom. His father said to him, "As soon as we get clear of this, you're going out again. I don't want you getting scared of the sea."

The sea and the island are inextricable, and together they pose the paradox of human will. I sat with Myron Tait, a Grand Manan Island fisherman, watching the tide come into a nearly empty cove of mud and sand. This was the Bay of Fundy tide, and it brought the fish that gave Tait his living. As he watched, it rose forty feet and its urgent strength pushed impatiently inward and upward, spilling into hollows, bustling clots of seaweed and scum before it.

"Once," Tait said, "I got fed up with the sea, and took a shore job. I was safe there and it was steady money. But then, on misty nights, I would hear those engines in the distance, the men coming in with their catch. I couldn't stand that. It nearly drove me mad. I went back to fishing."

Finally, and probably too late, the island proffers the last escape. I made friends with a man who had been around the world, had degrees from universities and shrapnel in his thigh from a Royal Tiger tank in Greece. He had come back to his island, and he talked about refugees he knew, men in flight from supermarkets and canned commercials and their own lives. They were a late phenomenon and were drawn from all over the world—an American scientist with a brilliant record in the United States, an English university professor ruined by a homosexual liaison with a student, an Irish nurse fleeing an unhappy love affair, a failed artist consoling himself with endless landscapes.

Their presence in Newfoundland was retreat and denial. They wanted to reduce the problem to its simplest elements and solve it. They ingratiated themselves with illiterate fishermen and old sea captains. They tramped the barrens, and caught salmon, and took their holidays in isolated villages.

Was my friend a refugee?

"I tell myself I'm not because I came back to help the people still stuck here. The twentieth century must come. I believe the island needs men to help ease these people into it."

He was reflective for a moment.

"And yet, am I that unselfish? Perhaps I am running from something. If I am, I don't know what it is."

The singing commercials have arrived. Uncle Benny will die. The fishermen will winter in Paris. The barrens will be plowed or forested. What to do? I heard some refugees discuss the problem.

"It won't be long before this place is ruined."

"Have you been to Labrador?"

"Yes, but there's nothing to do."

"What about Greenland?"

"Impossible."

For a generation, the island holds the two people: men going forward and men going back. I suspect both have missed the point somewhere. They will have to die with it not understood.

12

The Citadel of the Gulls

THROUGHOUT THE JOURNEY, I had traveled among gulls. They were so common, so much a part of the seascape, that they melted into it and became almost invisible. But the more I watched them, the more I was reminded of a human capacity to exploit and adapt. The gulls in constant contact with man were bold and aggressive; those in wild areas were withdrawn. They lived on Funk Island, but they also besieged fish-processing plants in voracious hordes waiting for opportunistic plunder. Everywhere, they had adjusted superbly to the place where they had chosen to live.

I watched a gull settle on the mast-top of a ferry going to Grand Manan Island and remain there, half-dozing, until we reached the island, whereupon he flew off rapidly. I could only assume that having found that the ferry took him to his destination, he had given up the unnecessary effort of flying to it.

On Bonaventure Island, there were always two, sometimes three, gulls who awaited the coming of tourists to the gannet cliffs. They stood, their bodies tense with expectation, as the clumsy humans stumbled down the grass slopes toward the gannets. They knew that sooner or later a tourist would disturb a gannet from her nest. Then, one gull would dart forward and steal the gannet's egg.

I watched gulls plunder a warbler's nest, steal food from other sea birds, feed on dead whales, and eat blueberries. They plagued the eiders and prowled puffin cities for unwary nestlings taking their first view of the outside world. I saw two fishing boats, one followed by hundreds of gulls, the other by none. When I queried my boatman about this, he shook his head. "We don't know how the gulls can tell the difference between the two boats," he said. "The boat with the gulls is going for cod. When the fish are gutted, there will be a feed for the gulls. The other is going lobstering. The gulls seem to know there will be no food from it. But how do they know the difference?" I looked at the two boats, but they were identical in appearance.

Gradually, the gulls forced me to think back to Kent Island, in the Bay of Fundy, which I had visited during the early part of the journey. I had not then believed it was possible to see anything fresh about sea birds which had been so well observed, photographed, researched, rhapsodized, and reviled by so many other people.

But as I traveled and unconsciously measured the gulls against the other forms of life, I realized I was guilty of a common human fault of dismissing the commonplace.

When I visited Kent Island, which contains the

largest herring-gull colony in North America, the fog was rolling in steadily and the hollow cry of Gannet Rock lighthouse lingered in the trees. As I listened, it was easy to believe that John Kent was still on his island. He has been seen on odd occasions walking through the trees, and once, in bright moonlight, he crossed the thick mud of a small inlet where, of course, he did not leave footprints. His wife became immortal in another way. She lived on the island alone after her husband's death, and when she died, an old woman, she put a curse on the island which drew many fishing boats to their destruction. No one has been able to live there successfully since her death in the late 1800's and the island retains an undeniable presence of the Kents.

The curse may have kept humans away but clearly it has had no effect on birds. My first night on the island, I stood in the open and listened. John Kent's steady footsteps sounded among the nearby spruces as he walked toward an old pit from which he used to quarry lime for mainland buyers. Kent was a supreme islander, a man who sought to sustain his independence in isolation. He must have been as comforted as I by the cries of the gulls from the southern end of the island, since they supplied him with an abundance of flesh and eggs.

As Kent's footsteps died, the first of the petrels arrived, and their wild cries suggested disorder and doubt. I had not been frightened by old Kent's ghost but I felt a touch of unease now. I recalled that the petrels are Mother Carey's chickens, the lost souls of dead fishermen who must spend eternity seeking land in darkness. Their stabbing cries were an unanswerable question:

Where? Where? Where-to-go?

Their swallowlike bodies were dim specters as they hastened overhead toward nocturnal assignations with their mates, waiting in several thousand burrows at the northern end of the island.

The arrival of the petrels provoked the gulls. I stumbled along a rocky shore and heard gulls and petrels, both diurnal birds, blundering among the spruces. A gull soared silently overhead, a wraith, and crashed into a tree. A squawling cry erupted and died.

Where? Where? Where-to-go?

Ooooooh G-a-a-a-w-d! the lighthouse cried.

Oy-oy, a gull said.

Along the shore, gulls caught petrels as they came in to land, caught them inefficiently, clumsily, haphazardly, but caught them. This ritual went on each night throughout the summer. I walked west toward the gullery and the petrel cries faded to become pinpoints of anguish in the dark.

I have a special feeling for gulls because they have adapted so ingeniously to man. They have survived in the Passamaquoddy region by establishing a citadel of more than sixty thousand creatures on Kent after having been driven off nearby Grand Manan Island by raccoons, foxes, dogs, and humans; and hounded away from the mainland by poison, shot, and nest destruction.

On Kent, for an idyll of summer, they become true islanders. It is the only time of the year they are safe; ahead lie fall and winter, storms, broken wings; the dispersion of some to Mexico, Michigan, Maine; hungry crowds of them prowling old fish plants; ice, blizzards, and long waiting times. It is little wonder that the summer gullery is raucous and copiously flowing with spirit.

I walked into a night world of swinging shapes, the crash of wings, aerial gasps, screams and groans. Gulls standing in open grassland sprang up and disappeared, and from the mist came a growing howl of accusation. Night walkers in the gullery were not welcome. I sat against a dead spruce and listened as the gulls, cackling and whistling, let themselves down blindly in the mist to return to familiar roosting places.

Ooooooh G-a-a-a-w-d! the lighthouse cried.

There is a human sound to a gullery. It is never silent. Cries and counter-cries suggest a purpose and a meaning to every second. Mist and darkness do nothing to inhibit the flow of action. Where was this gull going, a clumsy flail of wings, an awkward landing at my feet? Why this burst of laughter from a gull hovering directly overhead? What purpose in a gush of squealing cries down by the invisible shore? I listened and dozed away the night.

The moments before dawn are always special, but in this great gullery an inexpressible emotion involved both myself and the birds. The gulls felt it first. I was still drowsy, only half-conscious of that peculiar change which takes place in the air—or is it in the soul?—just before dawn. In darkness I heard muffled wings whisking overhead as though the birds were taking up pre-ordained positions to greet the light. I felt the tension, the anticipation of imminent events, the sense of purpose. I could swear I had mist-piercing vision.

The half-choked cries and whistles of the gulls changed abruptly in timbre. I realized suddenly that the mist had gone and bright stars shone overhead.

In one long exquisite moment before the perceptible beginning of day a wild cry came out of the night.

Koy-koy-koy-koy-koy, the voice cried, expressing the inexpressible: release from the suppression of the night, a salute to the dawn and to fellow gulls. The gullery responded with whistles and shrieks. Around me birds rose like ghosts, visible now with a faint iridescence which had sneaked into the gullery from no direction at all, and from everywhere at once.

Keer! the gulls screamed, and *koy-koy*, the voice cried, still lost in the gloom of the softly whispering sea.

Ha-ha, a gull cried, and *karraaaaaa*, another voice shouted high overhead. The tempo of the day quickened and birds swept purposefully overhead, no longer probing the darkness, but flying with rapid certainty.

The eastern horizon was just visible in an opalescent line of color when a herring gull made a strike about half a mile offshore.

Wheeee! he cried. I knew him. He was the schoolboy in a cherry orchard, and his message was unmistakable. Gulls in mid-air pivoted and turned toward him. As far as I could see in the dim light, birds shot into the air.

Ah-ha, one gasped over my head and plunged on out to sea.

Graaa, another screamed close behind. In the background, the horizon lightened rapidly. Its edge, a razorsharp line incised along the top of the sea, signified a spectacular dawn.

I could see the lone gull in the still sea, between island and horizon, wings upraised as he jabbed at young herring or shrimp. Gulls were silhouetted against the dawn, thickening in the air, as they converged on him. The gullery was in an uproar; several thousand birds hung screaming over it. Looking up, I saw them struck with color, brightened by a clinging light which glowed from inside them. They were flying in the real dawn that I could not yet see.

I turned toward the east again. Gulls plummeted untidily into the sea. The top of the sun appeared, and the dawn began.

Until this moment, I had forgotten I was an intruder. A few score gulls, with nests nearby, floated overhead or stood in trees and cried their objection to my presence; but most of the gulls were as yet unaware of me. Like an inadvertent witness of an intimate moment, I was inhibited. But it had to be done. I stood up.

Twenty thousand, thirty thousand gulls—who could count them?—rose in upflung curtains. It was a blizzard in reverse, an insane upset to the laws of physics. I leaned backward to see them all, stumbled on my heels, felt the weight and force of them. They were implacable. *Go! Go! Leave us alone!* Involuntarily, I turned and walked under them.

Birds were spread thinly over rolling green hillocks, far ahead of my long and searching shadow, but they were rising, marionettes in the wind, at my approach. At my feet, birds thrashed clear of long grass in which their nests were concealed. Hundreds beat out of a forest of dead, angulated spruces. The strident voices hammered home the message: *Enemy, enemy, enemy, enemy.* In response, a gull blundered out of the grass and, unsighted and confused, struck my thigh before turning away in flight downwind. The grass was drilled with corridors, escape routes from innumerable nests. An eider duck ran down one corridor, collided at an intersection with a fleeing gull. Both birds burst through the thin grass covering and took wing.

A nightmare quality infused the soaring gulls. I was in a great room filled with thousands of flying people who were venomously opposed to my purpose. I remembered fumbling a long pass in football once and being dismayed by the vicious growl from the crowd. No mercy might be expected. I was alone. On all sides, water glistened and enhanced my isolation. There was a collective will among these gulls which, for one panicky moment, caused my steps to falter, made me consider running. I mastered the impulse just as the systematic defense of the gullery began.

As I walked away from the sun, I caught sight of birds reflected inside my sunglasses. One of them became enormous. I turned and was buffeted by a rush of wind. Attackers fell on me, always from behind. I turned again and again, each time an arm's length from chisel beaks passing at forty feet a second. My face caused them to pivot sharply, and they hovered. I turned and walked. Down they came, silent until the last moment; then they gave a piercing whistle which, so close, drilled me clean through. Again, I wanted to run— goose-pimpled, intimidated. This was ridiculous! But I could not control the crawling feeling at the back of my neck.

At the same time, the splat-splat-splat of falling excrement signified another defense weapon. I would be hit soon. I lost control and ran like a kid, giggling, until I reached the crest of a rocky ridge where no nests had been built. The attacks stopped. The sun was white and stark. The gulls, the distant spruces, and the sun were a hiatus in time. I sat down and let the sight of it wash into me.

In this position, I was trapped in the center of the gullery, surrounded by nesting birds. I watched them hovering nearby, as if in wait for my flight; sharp eyes, down-turned beaks splashed with red at their tips, legs held loosely against their bellies. After half an hour, my distaste (or was it fear?) at confronting them again had diminished and I stood up and walked downhill.

The birds immediately took on specific identity. One bird approached from the west, turned in a ballooning climb, then attacked from the east, coming in fast and low, about waist level, then swerved upward to my face. Another bird hovered directly above me, then dropped with half-closed wings. In the reflex viewer of a camera, she looked like a bird of prey falling on her victim; a roar of wings at my ear and the gull shot away and pumped upward for another attack.

The attacks came increasingly close. I was struck twice on the head by gulls' feet. A small hammer rapped my skullbone and blood ran down my ear. A straddle of white spotted my sleeve. An egg, voided in desperation by an anxious mother, thumped down and burst open redly. I was struck squarely in the ear by a thick, evil-smelling mass of muck. Enough! I ran like a fool for the sea, leaped over rocks, plunged my head in icy water.

On the shore, I was able to watch the gullery without being directly attacked, merely harried. The community defense was much more complicated than it seemed. The defenders were not only attacking me; they were attacking other gulls who invaded their territory. A female, nesting at the shore, dived at my head, swerved up against the wind, and struck a hovering gull. She twisted and slashed at another bird flying nearby. The air space over me was divided and re-divided by the authority and territorial pride of the gulls. I was truly an interloper in this citadel; the rules of territory were rigidly enforced.

The sun had become a fireball against which the gulls wove intricate flight patterns. Its glare directed my attention to the ground, and instantly, I was in another world. Young gulls reacted to my arrival by walking up grassy slopes or stomping through long grass. Small groups gathered together. About forty thousand young- sters eyed me with the concern of the vulnerable.

I knew something about the dangers of their nesting life. Fewer than ten per cent would live to see the end of the year. If they survived the nest, the early juvenile days, then most of them would die, scattered across a hostile continent.

Once, I accompanied a group of ornithologists to a small Nova Scotia gull colony which lay on top of a flat, massive rock balanced at the edge of a cliff. The top of the rock was invisible, but its cap of gulls showed it must be densely nested. One scientist decided to climb to the top of the rock. He disappeared over its edge.

"Look out!" a colleague yelled. "They're jumping!"

The top of the rock was occupied by several hundred young, unfledged gulls. They had never seen a human before, and having nowhere to hide, they ran to the ocean side of the rock and leaped to safety. Safety? The drop was two hundred feet to bare rocks. Dumbly, we watched the plummeting bodies as all the jumpers, about a hundred nestlings, died. Such will to live, so sadly twisted, made the margin dividing life and death almost invisible.

Now, however, with no cover and no cliff, the young gulls seemed merely funny. Clumsily, they stomped away from me. Small nesting groups—two or three birds—jostled shoulders as they ran together. I laughed at their apprehensive, over-the-shoulder glances as they ran; laughed, that is, until I examined my photographs of them. The scope of their dilemma was revealed in every tense, anguished line of their bodies. Looking at the photos weeks later, I heard the cries again: *Enemy, enemy, enemy,* but this time, they were pleading.

I walked behind a fleeing nestling and his will collapsed. He huddled into the grass, head raised, submissive. I picked him up and he lay still in my hand. The strain of his body had gone. He accepted his fate.

But when I walked along the eastern shore of the island I saw a more mature reaction to danger. A few days before, Kent had been struck by a midsummer storm which had left crippled gulls behind it, many of them juveniles in their first or second year of life. I saw them picking their way over shore-line rocks. A flightless gull is almost surely doomed. As I walked, I fancied their emotions. This is anthropopathy, permissible for a writer if not for a scientist. I skirted a tidal pool and a one-year-old gull stood up in the shallows to face me. He made no attempt to fly. One of his wings hung down at his side but the carriage of his body was stiff, resistant to my presence. His head was erect, eyes bright. There was no suggestion of submission. He knew too much about survival to expect mercy, but his eyes expressed agony as they reflected his inability to flee. We looked at each other for a long moment, then he turned and walked away, each step a movement of doubt leading, as he well knew, nowhere.

I could not ignore the expression in that gull's eyes. It spoke to *me* as expressively as any word. I feel sorry for a man who will not indulge in anthropopathy. I recall spirited arguments I have had with a biologist friend who believes animals have no feelings, no thoughts, no doubts, no human attributes. He was anthropocentric, I told him, and arrogant. Was he sure that man was the central fact of the universe? Was all other life truly insignificant? I know, and he does not and that it is how we look at things that makes art. The art of life may be seen in the natural history of death.

I walked on, stumbling over thick ridges of rock, slipping among kelp and seaweed. To my left, set against the sun, gulls hung, watching. The crippled birds had disappeared into rock ravines or taken to the water to swim offshore and watch me. I came on a mature female gull, crouched down in weeds. She started heavily to her feet as I approached. Though she could not fly, her eyes were fierce and her posture hostile. Unlike the young gull with the broken wing, she had no doubts. She hated and mistrusted this enemy and wanted it gone instantly.

But even as she stumbled away a more powerful force was working in her. Her eyes dulled. She settled down on sand. I remained an hour, watching her. As her head drooped, she jerked it up angrily, then it drooped again as she slipped toward death. And yet, every time I moved, her furious spirit reacted. No submission, no fear, corroded her last moments. It was clear she was dying prematurely, clear that she understood this.

At midday, I felt I must digest the sight of the gullery. I was weary of being the object of so much rage and hostility. I walked from the foreshore back into the gullery and pushed through low bushes and thick grass until I was hidden. Hay Island slept beyond a full-risen tide. Grand Manan's blue shore crowded one horizon. In this geographic microcosm, I settled down, gull-like, and watched a leisurely and benign day slip away to the west.

Without haste, the gulls brought food back to their nestling youngsters. They were catching herring. From my observation point on a slight rise, I saw herring schools all around the island, dappling the surface of the water in broad patches of gray, disappearing and reappearing hundreds of feet further on. They were young fish who had formed into dense schools during the winter. Whenever they remained at the surface, the gulls streamed toward them; the movements became floods when the uprisings were thick.

At last, the sated gullery became still. Gulls stood in silent contemplation of the sea. I imagined a thousand crops filled with herring meat and wondered at the time it took to digest. Nearby, a gull twisted his neck, as if he were choking; then he vomited what looked like a ball of sodden feathers. It was the digested remains of a petrel, caught a few hours earlier. With digestion completed, the detritus was being disgorged. Then other gulls began to regurgitate and I witnessed the transition of herring, only partially digested, from sea to land. Gull necks writhed and twisted; young gulls crowded close, expectant. As the food rose in their throats, the adult gulls bent forward and down. At once, the nestlings stabbed at their beaks, grabbing at the first morsels. They squabbled among themselves over the food which spilled on the grass. The feeding was like a colonic spasm which began, completed its convulsive cycle, and rested. The entire gullery relapsed into sleep. As far as I could see, in every direction, gulls dozed as the herring entered the final, accelerated stage of the digestion process which would end, within minutes, among the grasses of the island.

The gullery day divided itself into periods of activity and sleep. As the birds came and went from the island, they revealed their moods and personalities. A large, handsome bird on a nearby log had an arrogant bearing. The stance of his body exuded health and confidence; his feathers gleamed; his eyes glowed imperiously. Here was a bird at the peak of his physical powers. I could feel his maleness.

When he flew away, another bird took his place on the log. He was a totally different character. He was older and less suspicious. When he saw me, he walked with mincing caution along the log to investigate. His manner was gentle, questioning. Who was I? What was I doing there? I had no answer. Even so, he remained unperturbed. He reminded me of an old shepherd I once knew who still rode at eighty-five. The shepherd flew like a gray bird in the saddle, and his eyes were peaceful. He was like an animal, so perfect was his containment in his world.

I looked at the gull, saw those same pacific eyes, and wondered whether he, too, was sinking into old age with acceptance. Were memories of his passionate, suspicious youth buried inside that small head? Did he recall the history of his island life? The gull gave me one last look and flew away.

Toward evening, a slow-building excitement ran up and down the shore lines, possessed groups of gulls who fled screaming out to sea. It sent some gulls pirouetting vertically, and their high shrieks found instant echo among the gulls on the island. A new spirit moved among the birds, a released and joyful energy. They flew wildly and without purpose.

At sunset, the atmosphere calmed and gulls flew silently. I walked toward the dead spruces, a forest of angular trunks and branches against the reddening western sky. Hundreds of gulls stood in these trees, balanced awkwardly on feet not adapted to perching on branches. I walked among the spruces as the sun dropped.

The horizon flushed crimson, light red, deep red. The sun was enormous. The gulls gathered around me as I sat, my back to a tree. They came down to me, no longer denying my presence but standing tall and quiet on any foothold they could find. A female came down within twenty feet of me. She craned her neck and said clearly, in an utterly feminine tone: *Gome.* I was silent. *Gome,* she said, pleading.

Would I go home? She flew six feet closer. We were almost eye to eye. She stood in the circle of the enlarging sun as it sank around her shoulders.

Gome.

Along the horizon gulls pumped energetically as they sought to finish the day's business before nightfall.

Gome.

The sun disappeared and the air chilled.

Gome.

She was perfectly right. Eggs were cooling; nestlings needed one last feed before sleep. My presence was an impossible imposition. I did not belong here another night. I got up and looked into her eyes. They *were* pleading.

Gome.

I walked back to my camp in the center of the island.

Around eleven o'clock, the wind now tumultuous in the spruces, I heard old John Kent stumbling along again. He faced another hard stint in the lime pit but the people on the mainland needed the lime and would pay for it.

As I warmed in my sleeping bag, the first of the petrels fled overhead in the wings of the wind.

Where? Where? Where-to-go?

I fell asleep and thought I knew the answer to their question.

13

The Long Road

THE ROAD TO THE ISLANDS stretches on and
the traveler ages. By this time, I had come
six thousand miles and I felt quite old. The
motion of travel had become steadily more significant
because, like it or not, I traveled at the *expense* of the
lives around me. I was heedless, demonic in my desire
to annihilate distance. The summer was short. The car
was fast.

An evening grosbeak flew through my side window,
whipped a sliver of skin off my ear lobe, and was killed
against the rear window. He was beautiful, a young
male in full breeding condition. Seeds oozed from his
beak. For a moment, I was sad, but the slow spruces
quickened, became a blur, and erased my thought that
in them was another grosbeak with a nestful of youngsters awaiting the dead bird's return.

I did not know this for sure, of course. I knew
nothing as I drove. It was only when I *stopped*, and
looked, and *listened*, that I understood anything. My
journey was more than half done before I realized what
was happening. I looked at expiring lives; beaks gaping
and stained with blood, last breaths gurgling in throats.

Memory flooded inward. Was I wrong to stop and witness? Was it better to plunge on and ignore the suspicion of cries left behind me?

Dawn, which usually found me traveling, was a time for death. It was the moment of awakening, and the creatures I drove among seemed as reluctant as I to adjust to the new day. Anonymous wings flashed out of thickets at the last minute. An owl flew at me, eyes gleaming, before he whisked to one side.

On a foreshore, overlooking a luminous mud flat that melted out of sight into mist, a heron took off and deliberately charged the car. I slowed but he came on, relentless. I braked savagely, disbelieving, but he went under the front of the car to the sound of a harsh rattle, like dried sticks being crushed. I got out. The heron was not dead, but he was crippled. He lay on the dark road in a sprawl of angular limbs and looked up at me.

At such an hour, the time of the firing squad and the hangman, the human spirit is low and pessimistic, and I felt terrible. This was neither sorrow nor compassion. Crippled or helpless creatures are common. Mercy killing is sophistry because it is a wish that painful death might not exist. But *I* had crippled this heron. He watched me with that secret knowledge wild creatures have about us. When I left him and drove away, we had satisfied our meeting. But my memory of it is a heavy one.

This closeness to death was like being a hunter again. It evoked unpleasant memories of shot rabbits and deer,

of squawking ducks and wounded quail. The memories
shuttled as I stopped near the body of another victim,
a wood thrush. Aspens whispered at my ear. I recalled
the first bird I had ever shot. I stole up on her, air gun
in hand, and squinted through my sights at one big
brown eye looking at me. She thought she was unseen
and knew nothing about another species of animal that
killed for fun. Now, twenty-four years later, I must
emphasize the indestructibility of that brown eye. I feel
no remorse; but that eye is still there.

A hare darted across the road and my locked wheels
must have missed him by the width of his whisker. I
poked about in the gloom, looking for a corpse, but he
had escaped. Another eye emerged from the past. A
rabbit ran up a hill and my rifle followed him, fired. He
fell with that odd relaxation of limbs of the drugged
and the dead. He rolled almost to my feet and looked
up, brown eye surprised, then he died.

The road twisted back and forth, and I was lost, I
was found, I was nowhere. I had to stop to know myself. A flooded lake and forest land fled past. The night
still hung heavily over the road. Mist whisked into the
headlights, then it was dawn. The air lit in a marvelous
luminosity, neither light nor dark, but a passionate suggestion of day.

The car was fast and quiet and the thrush too slow.
An agonized splay of wings in the headlights, then a
hollow sound. Death was instant. I stopped and got out.
The thrush was jammed in the grille, blood staining her

beak. Her feet were muddied and wet from walking along the edge of the sphagnum bog lake flanking the highway. She must have been hunting in semidarkness. On the flat metal under the grille lay a pale-blue egg, crushed where it had hit. A slow stream of yolk ran over the dew-beaded metal. The trees were filled with the sounds of thrushes singing into the new day. It does not matter that wild creatures have no feelings. We do. Somewhere in that predawn gloom, a nest awaited this bird, a voice called her.

The deaths on the road became a part of the journey, but for every adjustment I made to explain them, a new set of events twisted the meaning. In highland country, a partridge ran out suddenly: a double thump of the wheels. Death. I walked back to her crushed body, from which sprouted one tall and quivering feather.

A bright eye watched me from the long grasses beside the road—a bright eye, and *another* bright eye, and *another*. I was struck by the reality of her death. Crouched in the grasses were a dozen chicks, not more than a few hours out of the egg. Like all ground birds, they were fully ambulatory and could feed themselves. At least, they could feed if led to food. I looked at them, baffled. Were they orphaned? Could they carry on without their mother? Would the male partridge take over her duties? I turned away and drove a score of years down the highway.

Travel brought glimpses of creatures caught off guard by the hurtling time machine. A fox gliding in a flow of liquid motion across the highway. A lynx looking star-eyed at my quadrilights. A flock of sparrows fleeing desperately ahead of me through thick snow. A moose running in slow motion, then glancing over his shoulder like an uncle frowning at an ill-behaved nephew. He kicked up stones as I, in a broadsiding skid, found myself at his hindquarters. His feet flashed at my window. With a final effort, he pulled away and I was left in silence, my stalled car straddling the road.

In the cocoon of the car, the traveler is a fetus, warmed by the heater, comforted by the illusion of green instrument lights, the hiss of tires, and the soft thocking of wheels hitting the tarmac surface. Travel was seductive and hypnotic. Sheer motion became a reason to live. I floated down from a mountain into a red valley. I whisked into a bank of mist and heard the gasp of a tractor-truck's brakes. I swung, still in a dream, away from a tangle of green wreckage and a man's foot stuck out of a broken window. On a flat fast highway, I heard a sound like a steel drum being punched flat and saw dust blooming like the aftermath of an explosion. The cars huddled like wounded animals; passengers were flung into bizarre attitudes of injury and death.

After thousands of miles, my mind dulled. It could not adjust to the changing view, to the flood of messages received by my senses. In Newfoundland, particularly, the sensual flow became a flood—incomprehensible. Narrow, winding roads took me into new territories not of the earth. I drifted down a coast road into a blasted heath, so bare and empty that for a dozen miles I could not stop. Thousands of large white stones lay scattered across an undulating turf, dropped by a mischievous giant. I rounded a corner on the other side of the gulf and a gleaming expanse of inshore mud leaped to the eye; the same white stones were strewn across the tidal flats. What sort of game had that been, with the players a thousand miles apart?

In the end, every mile of the road suggested mortality. These maritime people are fatalistic. They know they must die; why not on the highway? They pass on corners and on the crests of hills. If they do not drive, they put on their darkest clothes, go out on moonless nights to walk in the middle of the road.

The traveler thinks he is in a world of order. But the highway is made to kill him, designed by engineers whose fees are the bodies of broken victims. Polished wood planking, wet, on a bridge, on a corner, on a sixty-mile-an-hour highway. The wrecks of three cars in one ditch. Wrecks in ditches, wrecks in lakes. The mind shuts off.

The motion of travel is delusive. I drove straight ahead for a year and never turned the wheel. A car skidded off the highway at sixty and careened across an open field. The driver and his wife sat upright, not moving a finger. A car pulled out and came toward me, undeviating. The driver and I examined each other's eyes before I rammed onto the shoulder and watched him pass; his eyes still retained my image, but he saw nothing.

I truly tried to see, but while motion was sustained it was impossible. I was caught in the hypnosis of my traveling, an emotion shared by many of my fellow travelers. A gravel road, a dust-spewing car ahead which must be passed. Why? No reason. Spirited vendettas on the straightaways, suicide pacts on corners and bridges. A driver from a place called La Belle Province swung across the road to prevent my passing him. He cannoned against me, knocked me onto the shoulder; below, a steep slope, a valley, rocks, trees. I accelerated desperately to pass and he hit me again, but in futility because he lacked an additional fifty horsepower which, accidentally, I possessed.

I was on lonely roads where, quite suddenly, there was no need to travel, no need to cover distance. I felt a sensuous ease. I dawdled. I stopped and listened for no reason. When I resumed traveling, I drove at a contemplative speed which, partially at least, enabled me to move and to see at the same time.

At this new speed, I rounded a corner on the loneliest road of all and saw a young bird standing, erect and watchful, in the middle of the road. My wheels locked and he disappeared. Shaken, I got out, reluctant to admit that I had been going too fast for a nonkilling traveler, and relieved to find that the bird still stood, now transfixed, under the front wheels. I picked him up. He was a young willow ptarmigan, an arctic bird which has been man-introduced to Newfoundland and which is flourishing. Almost immediately, a flash of red showed in the undergrowth and a female ptarmigan plumped down on the road in front of me. She circled me quickly with a soft cry; her mate appeared at the edge of the road and watched.

The ptarmigans wanted me to release the chick and to leave them alone. But I was a man and a meddler and I could not resist. The female was at my heel; as my feet twisted in the gravel, she ran around me and rested her chest on my toe. She looked up at me, head cocked on one side.

There are moments when man and animal can communicate so well that it seems like language. I reached down and picked her up. She, like the chick, was motionless and relaxed in my hand, and absolutely unafraid. Her eye was *regarding* me with an intent question in it. I cannot recall ever having received a more precisely worded statement from any creature. I put her down and released the chick beside her. They walked off into the barrens.

I drove away, ready to believe that the female, having exposed herself absolutely, left the male with his familial duty undischarged. Perhaps he sought to play his part too. He flew at my open window for a mile, following every curve in the road. When the whirr of his wings faded, I wanted to stop, turn back, go with the ptarmigans who might have become my friends.

14

The Underground City

GREAT ISLAND is Tahitian in form but arctic in substance. From a distance its peaked hills suggest a tropic paradise; but the waters around it are near freezing. It would not be a notable island except for one thing: It is hollow.

It was dug out by animals: they are birds but they seem homuncular to me. They have drilled its ground until it is as treacherous as a bog and as fluid as quicksand. Their manic energy makes them excavators, earthmovers, landscapers. They move soil as though there is pure joy in it.

Unlike the rowdy murres, the birds are silent and their movements imply collective will and intelligence. A quarter of a million of them patrol the high cliffs. On the day I arrived at the island, they stood at attention and watched the approaching boat. I had interrupted their excavating and they were hostile.

"Oh-ho," I shouted derisively, not to be intimidated by their displeasure.

The cry barked along under the cliffs. The birds were contemptuous; they made no response to the cry. But my shout penetrated the vitals of the island, and from its hollow center thousands of creatures appeared abruptly. A ripple of black-and-white bodies flew along the cliffs.

"Oh-ho!"

The birds were immaculate in black, white, and red livery, like dragoons, and with their military bearing went mass discipline. Their commander issued an order; the army moved. A division of troops streamed off a headland. The order was hastened down the coast. Other divisions leaped from the cliffs. The order went underground, and battalions appeared out of the earth, paused an instant, and jumped. A circus of flying machines, probably air cover for the retreat, erupted over inland hills. A new order was issued and the birds scattered. Within a minute, they were gone. The island was empty.

"Strange fellers, them puffins," said Jim Walsh, my boatman.

The puffins of Great Island form the largest colony of their kind anywhere. Of all sea birds, the puffin is the most appealing to non-bird-lovers. He is duck-sized and his conical, brightly colored beak sprouts from his face like a big chisel; he looks perpetually astonished, though I suspect his emotion is ill temper. He is an auk, a close relative of the murres, and of the great auk. But for a reason lost in heredity, the female must burrow to lay one white egg a year. Great Island is easy to dig and draws the puffins of the northwest Atlantic to it every summer.

The puffins do not want people on their island, and they have methods of keeping them away. I tried to land a dozen times, but each time I was thwarted. The puffin commander has a treaty with the elements. He ordered a swell out of a calm sea. Another time, a squall nearly drowned me when I was within a handhold of the island's rocks. On the third occasion, the punt broke down and it was three hours before we were rescued. Finally, I reached the island near dusk with Jim Walsh. The water swished against black rocks. The wind was rising.

"Hurry!" Walsh said.

I leaped into the womb of night and jarred bone as I landed. The punt backed away and dissolved. Did the people of the island sleep, or did they wait at the top of the cliffs to roll rocks down on intruders? I struggled for an hour to carry my equipment to the top. As I climbed, the night life of the island began. Gulls sailed overhead in gray blurs. A lone petrel cry lit the blackness with a tiny light. The wind increased. By the time I had my gear at the top of the cliff, it was a near gale. A huge moon rose, writhing with mist.

Despite the moon, I was lost. All I knew was that I must get away from the cliffs before I could sleep safely. Dusky hills rolled inland, patched with scrubby trees. I loaded my packs, hoisted them, and stepped forward cautiously. Immediately, I was falling; the weight of my packs drove me two feet into the earth. I staggered up, stepped forward, and fell again. The earth growled and moved under my cheek; an agonizing pain shot through my hand as I was bitten by a puffin. The angry bird, buried under my clumsy fall, struggled to be free of the burrow.

The island fought me, foot by foot, until, exhausted and dispirited, I reached level ground. This time, I let myself fall. When I hit the ground, it collapsed again and I went down, pack and all, into loose earth. Before going to sleep, I heard petrel cries sparkling downwind. Near me, a puffin who resented my presence on the island, gave a subterranean growl.

I awoke by opening one eye. The other eye was buried in damp soil. The pack straps had bitten off circulation in my arms, and needles shot through my veins. I looked up into the dim light at a man standing over me. He was an extraordinary-looking fellow, ugly; well, God! Frightening! I lurched up and the puffin flew away.

My eyes rose above ground level and I saw a horde of silent people. I stood up, Alice-in-reverse, dripping soil. I shucked the packs and started to walk.

The digging of the puffins is so methodical and orderly in its exploitation of the ground that I expected to find an artifact: a digging tool, a tiny shovel, or a wheelbarrow. The puffins use their clawed paddle feet to dig the earth like pioneer farmers exploiting soil. They attack any area suitable for digging, whether it is open, forested, or hilly, and their tunneling soon kills everything except some hardy grasses.

Their riddling of the earth is so intensive that soil

is moved by the acre. Along many of the cliff edges the top layer of soil, well grassed, was gliding gradually toward the edge as its underpinnings were dug out from beneath it. In places, earth and grass overhung the cliffs, soft green icing sliding off a cake.

I walked into a new metropolis; the soil was flung up, black and glistening as though from a plow. Beyond it was the site of an older occupation, where the trees and shrubs were beginning to die. Beyond that again was a deserted city. The soil there had a different character, oddly unsubstantial, as though its organic matter had been leached out of it as a result of the incessant digging.

The deserted cities were miniature Pompeiis. Thick growths of grass and fresh-sprouting shrubs and trees only partially concealed the assymetrical lines of corridors, of ceilings long since fallen in, of collapsed galleries, of cross-shaped lines of tunnels that intersected and branched like the veins of a leaf.

Such abandoned puffin cities are going through a process of rehabilitation. This course of occupation, desertion, and reoccupation has been going on for thousands of years, as the puffins, the grasses, the trees, and the shrubs move back and forth across the exploited earth.

The burrowing seems aeons separated from the activity of any flying creature. I looked up and saw that the puffins had paid a price for their excavating abilities. They flew badly. Their stability control, particularly when they were flying cross wind, was poor. As the birds turned over my head, flying across a light wind, I could see them rocking and yawing slightly. Many of them, seeking control as they slowed, thrust down their feet the way an airplane lowers its flaps. The paddles trimmed the flying machine, slowed flight, and enabled the puffin to fly hard against his own air brakes. I looked down from a cliff and saw a puffin darting along underwater, using both feet and wings, literally flying underwater, to catch a fish. Farther offshore, a group of puffins half flew and smashed repeatedly into oncoming waves, the collisions sending them ricocheting upward but doing nothing to stimulate them into real flight. Was I seeing evolution in action, the development of a flightless creature?

I reached the highest point of the island and had an unobstructed view of land and sea around me. During the climb, the wind dropped abruptly, brought a friendly reminder of another zone of climate as it veered halfway around the compass. The air cleared of birds; they disappeared from cliff-tops, ducked back into burrows, or dropped down to the water. As I watched, about ten thousand of them, fluffs of cotton wool, gathered in the light swell near the foot of some cliffs. They were spectators now, not hostile creatures. They wanted some justification for my presence. I felt very tall and powerful, standing so high above them. They were a great audience. I remembered thousands of people waiting equally expectantly for the start of Australian outdoor symphony

concerts. Perhaps I was a performer. With this childish
fancy implanted, I roared out a bar of *Godunov*. The
singing rattled and bounced back to me with double
and triple echo which was still returning to me when
the audience began to applaud.

It started as scattered clapping, then spread to become a full-throated tattoo of sound, twenty thousand
wings beating on the water as the puffins took off. They
lifted, leaving diverging, crisscrossing tracks, and the
applause died abruptly on the briefest opera career in
history.

I walked down the hill; a low overcast was gathering. It was a typical Newfoundland day: a trace of mist
flying across the water, a touch of warmth abroad, a
glowing light breaking through the clouds. The sun
threw down a column of light, and the puffins were on
the move again. The birds had settled about half a mile
offshore, thinly spaced across several hundred acres. A
space empty of birds was growing in the middle of them,
yet no birds, I was sure, had flown. Along the edge of
the cleared area, birds disappeared with sharp flips of
their bodies. A school of fish, perhaps working its way
up the coast to spawn, was the target. The puffins, I
knew, were diving *under* the school to make their attacking runs upward putting the fish at a disadvantage.
The fish could only flee to the surface and there was no
escape there.

A precise and disciplined organization activated the
puffin hordes. Hundreds turned to face the hunting area,

aware that prey was there. Applying the power of wings and kicking feet, they rose like small fighter planes, rocking back and forth as they sought equilibrium, falling into precise formations—vees and in-line-asterns—and headed toward the empty space of water.

Within seconds, the first wave of attackers skidded on the sea. They dived so quickly that the pencil-thin marks of their landings remained engraved on the water for a moment after they disappeared. A second wave of puffins, farther off, responded to the hunt, took off, twisted back and forth, though not yet sure of their destination.

By this time, five or six thousand birds were underwater and the scene was confused by countless circling birds. As far as I could see, none of the original divers had surfaced. Abruptly, fish broke the surface at several points. Puffins surfaced among them and took off, heading for the island.

I felt like the batman on an aircraft carrier; I had to flag these flying forms down to the flight deck. Beyond the approaching birds, the hunting area was busy with thousands of birds, diving and surfacing. Fish leaped, roiled acres of sea.

The first divers swept overhead, trailing wisps of small fish from their beaks. They turned out to sea, tightening their formation, then came roaring back over the island. Members of the squadron fell away to land and disappeared underground.

I looked offshore again and saw another flight of

puffins heading toward the island. They hung in the air, and I had a pang of memory, going back more than twenty years. A friend of mine, Jack Oughton, once attacked the battleship *Tirpitz* at such low altitude the ship's main guns could be aimed and fired at him. He saw the groups of shells coming at him, "fat, black pigs." I watched the puffins coming at me and felt a shiver as I saw intelligent purpose at work and the little pigs flung accurately at their target.

The massive movement of birds ended. They disappeared with such ease I doubted I had seen them hunting at all. The island was empty again. The sea was bare. I walked down toward a cliff, settled myself in a hollow, and dozed.

I awoke to an uproar. Gulls screamed; their cries galvanized the puffins. Groggy, I sat up while puffins poured out of their burrows in thin streams. Thousands of them rose from offshore positions to join the birds sweeping over the island. They formed a flock which swept around in a great half circle, turned across a cove, and rose high. For a second, the flock was motionless, like a structure built up from the cliffs. Then the structure toppled toward me. A flashback to childhood and cowboy movies and I had an impulse to scream: "Look out! Here they come!"

A mass of birds planed diagonally across the wind, dropped to sweep along the cliffs where I stood. Their numbers and the odd, sideways movement was illusive and made it seem that the birds were still and the island was moving. I toppled to one side in an effort to preserve my balance. The puffins were hostile again. I must begone. They streamed past in silent flight that was more menacing than any amount of screaming. On they came, cold blue eyes staring, red feet stabbing the air for balance. One bird stopped in mid-air six feet away, held motionless by the force of the wind and turned his head to look at me. I could hear the wind rushing through his wing feathers. He retracted his feet and rejoined the birds pouring overhead. In a few moments, the flock passed and made a wide sweep out to sea. Back it came toward the cove, rose to its toppling height, and fell, fell toward me again.

The circling birds were a fraction of Great Island's puffin population. Far out to sea, thousands of them dappled the water. Distant cliffs, beyond the cove, were covered with more watching thousands. A second huge flock was maneuvering over an island peak. Mist darkened the horizon. I sat down heavily and the ground collapsed around me.

To the north was a vision of primeval splendor. The island swept down into the sea in a running rage of motion, and its shore rocks bucked under water in a soft ululation of surf. The peaks of the land disappeared into thick mist.

The puffins did not want to be lost in mist. The hollow island's warm caverns beckoned them: Come home, wanderer, come home to the hollow island and be safe.

They came out of the sea in their legions: silent,

intent, humorless. There was no idle, circling flight now. They landed immediately in a blur of short wings, disciplined parachute divisions dropping accurately on target. In the mist sounded croaks, clashing wings, grunts and growls, like the noise of men struggling in a football scrimmage. Far off sounded the engine of a boat coming to pick me up. I took a final look down the coastline, fast disappearing in the amorphous mist, and saw several thousand kittiwakes and gulls appear out of the sea and settle along the black rocks of the shore. The island was alive with a *presence* I could not describe.

At that moment, unseasonably and unexpectedly, a deep-throated roar of thunder came out of the mist. I admit I am more impressionable than the next man, but I swear that sound was pure sorcery. The puffin commander's elemental spirit had spoken. Who, except a truly modern man, pragmatic and realistic, would deny the presence of a god out there?

Moments later, he deluged the island with rain, and I carried his cold fingers in my collar back to the mainland.

15

The Lonely Children

THE MOMENT THE TRAVELER stops in this island world of mine, the children appear. They are silent, watchful, and shy. They stand in the shadow of a yellow frame house, dark eyes thoughtful; they watch you on leaning wharves, or from perches on lobster traps or piles of salmon netting. They look normal, well dressed for the most part, neat and clean. But they are not normal, at least not in our terms. They are island children. Watching them, you may see some of the secret of the island character and perhaps get another insight into man himself.

The longer my journey, the more the children intruded. The summer was mature and its end was suggested by days of passionate heat which could not last. I was almost at the end of a journey, and I looked back at those who were just beginning one.

The children of the islands, their roots much deeper in the past than mine, are caught in a collision of time. They are trapped between their anachronistic parents, who may not read or write, and the world they know from movies and television: jet planes, hydrogen bombs, Sophia Loren, and vehicles heading for Mars.

They can never be like mainland children. Their sense of the outside world is a fairy-tale one. Jack climbs the beanstalk in those far-off cities; buildings are fifty miles high. One youngster, living in a village of a hundred people, said: "New York is a place *twice* as big as here."

I felt their frustration, sometimes their rage, even among those of little education and with no experience of the outside world. They sensed an intolerable situation. They betrayed themselves with a definable quality. They were old-young, shy-bold, keen-dull: schizoid.

They looked at me and they knew me as a spirit, but they were baffled by me as a man. They wanted information. They gathered silently around me as I parked my car on the banks of a tickle, and they looked with the disquieting, indirect attention of shy primitives. Their ignorance could not be admitted. I greeted them cheerfully, but they did not respond. They just watched. One stroked a door handle of the car and I heard him whisper to another youngster: "It's a Yankee."

Silently, three boys got into the car. They rubbed the dashboard instruments, the knobs, the seat belts.

"Aye," one of them said, "he's a Yankee, all right."

Shy? Two of them got into the back seat and brought out my camera bag.

"Cahn we 'ave a look?"

I nodded.

Two others worked away at polishing the hubcaps

of the car with grass. I was surrounded by twenty intent faces.

"What are you going to do when you grow up?" I asked the oldest-looking youngster. He was about nine; he looked astonished. Nobody had asked him *that* before.

"Oi doan' know, moi son," he said paternally. This disposed of any chance to have a straight, man-to-boy colloquy, so I made my next question general.

"Do you like living here?"

There was a muttered conference in which I heard "What 'e say?" Then, affirmative head-nodding.

"How would you like to go to St. John's?" I asked, mentioning the island's capital, which was three hundred miles to the south.

They conferred again. Again the mutterings, and this time, there was partial affirmation, but some doubt.

"How would you like to go to New York?"

This baffled them. They whispered together and shook their heads. Then their leader spoke: "Nar, sir, oi doan' reckon we would."

"Where's Europe?"

A complete blank; the question not even worth considering.

"Where's England?"

A blank again; then a small-old voice from the back: "That's whar the Queen are."

"Where's America?"

Absolute agreement; they all pointed south.

"Dahn thar!"

But they were restive at the questions. They wanted to know about me. One of them was stroking a camera case. "Dis be one of dem Yankee cameras?" he asked, hopefully.

"No, Japanese."

He was disappointed. They were all disappointed. I had lost face. But he persisted. "Dat's one of dem powerful Yankee cars?" he asked, pointing to my car.

It was the same car any Newfoundlander could buy, but I began to get the drift of things now. "Yes, very powerful."

This reassured them. They grinned at one another. Now, that was something to think about, a "powerful *Yankee* car." He persisted. "How fast would she go, sir?"

"Two hundred miles an hour."

They were delighted. They nodded knowingly. The leader spoke again, shaking his head. "We doan' have cars that fast here, sir."

Later, if these children are unlucky, they will undergo an unpleasant transformation. They will lose their naïveté. They will become tough and assertive—not knowing quite what to be assertive about, nor with whom. In an urban part of the island, I was watched by a group of youngsters as I walked down the street. They laughed as I passed.

" 'E's got some *fancy* walk on 'im!"

In that time of their lives, the mainland world is strange enough to be frightening and they know enough about themselves to resist it. I traveled with a youngster making his first trip to the mainland and he was terrified. I tried to reassure him but he was inconsolable.

"It doan' matter what ye say, sir, oi doan' loike it!"

But before they become knowledgeable, the children are caught, like insects in amber, for observation. I found myself a hundred miles from anywhere, in a village so isolated that I was reminded of the hitchhiker on the driveway and the story of his broken arm. I had wanted to climb a mountain behind the village—a towering mass of rock cliffs about a thousand feet high—but I was unsure of the steep track up the hill. Would some of the village youngsters guide me?

The adults were doubtful. "Who would talk to '*im*?" meaning me. They thought.

"Billy, 'e might."

But Billy, aged thirteen, would have nothing to do with me. He peered from behind a shade in a small house and would not come out.

"Then 'ow about Joey?"

Joey would not talk to me, or look me in the eye, but he would lead the way up the hill. We tramped along narrow boardwalks between houses painted yellow, blue, green, white; through chickens digging in trash and young pigs scavenging on garbage. As we walked, we picked up other youngsters, equally silent, who walked serpentine ahead of me.

For the next hour, as we climbed among clouds clinging to the sides of the overhanging cliffs, no word was exchanged. I tried questions, songs, jokes; nothing worked. I stripped off all my clothes on the banks of a mountain tarn and swam in the peat-brown water. The children looked at me and smiled faintly. They *knew* I was mad.

We looked down on the village, a cluster of tiny houses, but the sight provoked no comment. The boys did not talk among themselves but sat, composed and watchful. They were simply not reachable.

These older children, the teenagers, reveal another countenance of island childhood. They are the survivors of diphtheria epidemics, plagues of whooping cough, scarlet fever, and tuberculosis. Even today, gastroenteritis is a dreaded killer. German measles was often epidemic and caused many blind-deaf children when it struck pregnant women. In some villages, inbreeding has been going on for more than two hundred years and the children are its history.

In one village, long since deprived of teachers, clergy, or doctors, I was surrounded by a group of idiot children, or so they seemed during my first look at their gaping mouths, the dribble running down their chins, the running sores on their legs.

"Hello," I said dubiously to the eldest child, a gangling girl of twelve. She did not respond but looked stonily at me. Next to her, an eleven-year-old boy (or was he eleven? or was he a boy?) was sucking his thumb. He trailed a dirty piece of rope to the end of which was tied a tattered copy of the *Ladies' Home Journal*. God alone knew what it represented. Next to him was an eight-year-old girl who had vomited recently; much of it still dripped down the front of her dress. The children were filthy and I did not care to look closely at their matted, dirty hair.

"Hello," I said again, and this time I drew a reaction. The eldest girl began to laugh. She said something incomprehensible to one of the others and the laughter spread. Soon, they were all doubled over, howling with glee and pointing at me between bursts of laughter. It was not pleasant laughter. It had the bitter edge of desperation about it, which came from their fear and incomprehension of the dark stranger.

Later, I talked to a clergyman about these children. He shook his head.

"The inbreeding there is awful," he said. "The government should ship the entire village away, split it up. That would be an end to it. And not a moment too soon."

But most extraordinary of all, each village produced different kinds of children. In one village, the children were clean, friendly, polite; in another, they hid from me. In an unkempt village, I watched a dog, a small pig and a twelve-year-old boy rooting through some scrap of rubbish together; in a spotlessly clean village, a well-dressed thirteen-year-old told me seriously he hoped to be educated at Harvard. Both were fishermen's sons.

In one village, so isolated by rock and ravine that no road will ever reach it, I walked along the street, sidewalk, footpath, whatever I might call it, and saw a blonde girl watching me. At first, I thought my eyes had misled me; it is unusual to see stunningly beautiful women in these villages. But she was not only beautiful; she had star-dusted radiance that caused one's breath to catch.

Usually, the shyness of the village youngsters sends their eyes away from yours, but this girl kept looking intently, no, *invitingly,* at me. As she watched, she changed the position of her body slightly, an incredibly subtle movement, so provocative it forced me to look from her face to her body. It was not a child's body, though she was a child, thirteen at the most. She was barefoot, dressed in what looked like a burlap bag cinched around her tiny waist. Long golden hair cascaded down her back and bosom.

"Come with me," she said when I was close. "Come with me."

I halted in astonishment.

Both her body and her voice invited me. "Come with me," she pleaded, half turning away. "*Come* with me."

A woman appeared at the door of a nearby house. Like a hawk leaping on her prey, she swooped out and with one hand seized the girl's arm; with the other, she smashed her over the side of the head. The girl fell and was half dragged away into the house. In that last glimpse of slender thigh and dragging ankle, I saw her now strangely contorted face and understood the pathetic mismatching of her Circe's body and her poor, idiot brain.

Almost every small Newfoundland village has its

share of "dummies"; children born deaf and, therefore, mute. Until recently, nothing much was done for such children. I saw a six-year-old boy-dummy row a dory weighing a quarter-of-a-ton in pursuit of half a dozen boys in a skiff. They had wronged him in some way, and as he rowed, he screeched his fury like a magpie. Spittle and foam flew from his writhing lips as he sought to expel the demons of frustration inside him.

The island children may be frustrated for many reasons; living so far from a railroad, or even a road, or a movie theater, or having never traveled in an airplane, or having seen television, yet knowing that all these things exist. They have the desire of all youngsters to escape, but it is multiplied a thousand times by their isolation.

I had just finished work at dusk at a Newfoundland scientific research station when I heard a soft whistle. I looked toward the road, about fifty yards away, and saw two girls standing at the entrance to the station. In what I thought was a reasonably friendly response, I whistled back. The two silent figures regarded me.

"Whatcha doin'?" a voice said.

"I was just finishing work," I said, feeling foolish. "What are *you* doing?"

"We're walkin'," the voice said. There was a long pause.

"Why doncha come out here?" the voice asked.

I am susceptible to women and have had more than my share of disaster as a result. But nothing in my nature or experience told me what to do in this situation. I was free of my responsible city life, was I? Well, here was an opportunity to test it. But I hesitated.

"I'm not quite through," I said, temporizing.

"C'mon," the voice said relentlessly, instantly divining my weakness.

"Look," I said. "*You* come in here."

"Are you comin'?" the voice said, sure of itself now.

Years of metropolitan suspicion held me back. What were the Newfoundland rules when a young woman attempted to pick up a total stranger at dusk? According to my experience of the city, it meant either prostitution, which this could not be, or the prelude to a mugging, which was equally unthinkable in this rural place. Yet the connotation was unpleasant, not to say sordid. I could not reconcile that with the gauche young voice in the dark.

Curiosity resolved all. I would pick her up in half an hour at the crossroads at the bottom of the hill. I would drive her home. But, still being suspicious, I would take a companion with me, a young research worker, Dave, who would fit into the group as a companion for the other, silent girl on the road.

Dave and I cruised downhill thirty minutes later, and when the low-beam headlights picked out their legs, Dave said suddenly: "How *old* are they?" Then they were out of the headlights, the back door was slipped open and they both slid into the car. One of the girls froze against the seat and was not a part of the gathering. The other girl put both forearms on the front seat and leaned forward. Her face, lit by the glow of instrument-panel lights, was not only a close copy of Debbie Reynolds; it was also the face of a very young girl. Dave was shocked. "You must be pretty young," he said.

"You can take us home now," the girl said coolly. "Straight down this road."

Both girls were twelve. Both lived with their parents and went to school. They walked the roads—I was reminded of Italy, Greece, Spain and its nocturnal crowds on the roads—every night. They walked between five and fifteen miles a night, ranging in every direction they were likely to meet people. They were driven home every night, "well, *nearly* every night," by a cross section of the community—youngsters with cars, farmers, young married couples. They had walked to the research station deliberately because they had heard there was a stranger there.

"What were you thinking of when you stood on the road and whistled?" I asked.

"Think?" She was puzzled. "We wanted you to come out and talk to us."

"But you didn't know who I was, how old I was, or anything," I said. She shrugged. Apparently, that was supremely unimportant. I asked her what interested her most.

"Boys."

What was she going to do when she grew up?

"Grow up? I'm grown up now."

Was she scared at being in an automobile with two strange men?

"No. Why should I be?"

Did she want to go away and see the world?

She shrugged.

See New York?

Shrug.

Hollywood?

"Oh yes. And see all the stars. Have you ever seen a star? Gregory Peck? Elizabeth Taylor?" The questions tumbled out.

Did she read?

Shrug.

What music did she like?

"That's some nice radio you've got," she said. The radio was playing a delicate adagio movement in a Corelli suite. Did she like that sort of music?

Shrug. "No."

Suddenly, "You can stop here and let Helen out." Helen disappeared silently down the jet-black road.

"Turn right here. You can stop now."

No house was in sight and I realized these nocturnal excursions were illicit.

"Well, good-by." She got out, but Dave reached through the window and grabbed her arm. "Not so fast," he said. "Do we see you again?" She nodded.

"When?"

"Tomorrow night," she said without hesitation.

"Where?"

"We'll walk again."

"Can't we pick you up?"

"No. Tomorrow."

She disengaged her arm and walked up the road in the headlights. She had pretty legs and the lines of her body made her look adult. We shared the guilty feeling of our innermost thoughts.

"I suppose there's a law against this sort of thing," Dave said. Then he laughed. "Oh boy, they sure start early."

As we drove back to the camp, he talked about his youth. He had been brought up on the mainland, in a rural area almost as lonely as this. He knew what drove that girl out on to the roads every night. He knew about girls who must stay at home and boys who must leave.

When she, our night flower, had heard there was a mainlander nearby, she knew what to do. She was already competing, in her way, with teenage girls who had boyfriends with automobiles and money, and she knew what she wanted. But the child in her could not know the consequences. I had a chilling memory of young gulls who knew what *they* must do, escape, run from the danger, knowing nothing of the endless fall into the abyss.

"What will happen to her?"

I had half hoped that the prognosis would be good and that the rules might be elastic enough to allow this girl her escape, without the fall. But no. Soon, she would meet somebody. Why not? She was looking for him. The male might be a knowledgeable teenager, but more likely, he would be a lumber-camp worker or a stranger. She would probably get pregnant. All this would happen *before* she had anything more than instinctual judgment; it would be disastrous even though her parents would likely condone her behavior.

Dave, being closer to a liaison with the girl, was thoughtful and silent. I, the stranger who would be gone tomorrow, was absorbed by an illumination of the naked female, a huntress prowling those island roads in search of a life.

16

A Night with Mother Carey's Children

RAIN BEGAN TO FALL heavily soon after dusk, and the island streamed with mist which expanded my flashlight beam into a glowing explosion of light. Finally, I was on Gull Island, the last island in the journey, the singing island of my dreams, the summation of a summer and of an idea.

Under my feet, the creatures of the island awaited the night. Far out to sea, their mates were heading through the mist and darkness for the island, this superb refuge. I felt their approach on my tingling skin.

During the day, I had explored the island. It was unspectacular, less than half a mile long, rising steeply on all sides to a wooded ridge of spruces, and honeycombed, at its southern end, with puffin burrows. But the puffins were insignificant, a scant few thousand.

Almost all the island was drilled with tiny holes scarcely big enough for me to insert my hand. In places, there were three or four burrows drilled in every square yard of ground. They were everywhere: under tree roots, in thick grass, on bare earth slopes, half-concealed

among leaves. If I had not known these were the burrows of tunneling birds, I would have suspected the
existence of an enormous population of rats or weasels.

In the deep parts of the spruce forest, toward the
crest of the ridge, the burrows were so numerous I could
smell the petrels inside them. The smell was musky, the
odor of the oil they exude. In this place of ruined
branches and filigreed twigs, it was overpowering. I put
my ear against the earth in an effort to hear the subterranean creatures, but the earth was silent as the grave.
What did the petrels do as they waited in the dark? Did
they listen for the first cry of their mates? Did they know
when darkness covered the island?

The mist came inshore in waves over a sable twilight
sea. To my surprise, I was trembling slightly, though I
was not cold. The spruces dripped as the darkness grew
up out of the sea, rose to my knees, and blotted out my
last view of gulls sliding through the mist.

The petrels, through millennia of bitter experience of
being hunted by gulls in daylight, do not come near
their island immediately it is dark. They allow the night
to mature and deepen in such full measure that the
night-crying gulls are quiet and the island seems completely asleep.

Water seeped down my spine. The first cry rang out
overhead. Until the voice of a petrel is heard, it is impossible to conceive of any wild sound so charged with
exuberance, so human in its joy and expectation. No
other sound resembles it; no sound is so thrilling. I lis-

tened as mist washed sibilantly against my straining eyes.

The petrels are not nocturnal; I knew they came to the island able to see only as well as I could. On a night like this, how would they see anything? Another cry sounded *chack-chack-chack—er—ell!* and the cry was caught up by others, deeper in the mist: *Chack-chack-CHACK—er—ELL! Chack-chack-CHACK—ER—ELL!*

The cries twisted, came close, receded, and silence interposed. *They* were out there; I could feel them, a collective presence. How many? Where?

Chack-chack-chack—ER—ELL!

A bird cried at my ear, and I turned in time to see a dim shape flee away. Another call echoed in the cathedraled vault of the mist, then a rush of calls, some behind me, above, in front. A bird struck me on the head, was gone. Silence. Mist whispered a secret. What? What was that? Nothing.

Nobody knows how the petrels find their island. But they are wary of it; they need the comfort of numbers before they are ready to land on it. Far distant, a flurry of calls, then silence again. But the moment was building; I could feel it. A cry swept in front of me, beginning on my far right, crescendo in front of me, diminuendo on my left, then fading into the mist. The cries took hold, became authoritative, numerous and encouraging. They formed layers, one atop the other, voices crying to a listener in a canyon. *Chack-CHACK-chack-chack-chack — ER — ELL-CHACKCHACK — er — ELL-CHACK!*

The movement of sounds laced the air with sculptural patterns that had breadth, depth, and a spell of shape and passion. Their physical reality made the sounds a part of a solid universe.

The petrels drew confidence from their audacity and lowered themselves. I saw shapes whisk against the faint glow of the night: long-winged shapes, sharp-pointed, graceful in their lunging eagerness to cover distance. Only an ornithologist could think of them as petrels. They are Mother Carey's chickens, as sailors believe, truly sea swallows.

I fired my flashlight upward and a petrel hovered in its beam like a giant black butterfly, then jerked away. Another bird hit my head and knocked my cap over my eyes. Another struck the flashlight, got entangled in my camera strap, and lunged free. I played the flashlight beam and caught a petrel briefly, but he flew too quickly to be held. A bird struck me in the face with surprising force. Another flew into my open windbreaker, racketed around my back while my fingers reached for him, was gone as suddenly as he had come.

I walked; I stood; I was dazed. It did not matter where I looked, the petrels were settling and blundering. Their cries mingled with the clashing of wings in branches, with sudden flurries of movement in the grass. I imagined they were trapped, entangled, but the moment my flashlight beam lit, they were momentarily visible, black eyes staring, graceful wings cocked high, and then gone.

The cries, the proximity of the birds, the spectral

speed of their flight, was intoxicating. But it was an ecstatic inebriation few men are privileged to experience. I became hypersensitive. So strongly did I long to know these shimmering creatures that I wanted to reach out and scoop in armfuls of them, to hear their cries against my cheek, to feel their soft wings beating close to me, as though I were a child. It *was* childish. But I had surrendered myself to the knowledge that this was a mad and magic night.

I reached out and did, in fact, scoop petrels out of the air. One hovered in front of me and fanned my cheeks enticingly. I took her in my hands and the wings stilled instantly. She lay in my hand and revealed a dusky, lithe body, eyes bright and unafraid (how long ago that willow ptarmigan, also quiet in my hand?) The peculiar tube-nose sprouted from the top of her beak, her delicate black papyraceous paddle feet half clenched. Then she recognized hostility and flexed her wings to be free. I released her.

The petrels poured through the island air. They spun out of the mist, laughed madly, hurled themselves into the trees, and fled away. I caught a score of them, but I was afraid to walk. Birds now so well covered the ground that I could not take a step without the risk of crushing them underfoot.

It was midnight and the petrels had, within an hour, transformed the expectant island into the dance ground of a Bacchic orgy. The singing and dancing were not the expression of absolute abandon, though. They had purpose. While the air was still filled with yodeling cries, a new sound intruded. It was subterranean and came from a single point immediately under my feet. Then it sprang from a dozen places.

I have found it difficult to describe the petrels' aerial sound; their underground cry *is* indescribable. It was delicious, sensuous: a rich, throaty warbling of ineffable joy and pleasure, a delighted salutation for the wanderer returning from the sea. I saw the petrels fall at my feet, each one kicking clumsily toward a single welcoming burrow where a mate waited, then heard the sound of the greeting. It was a human emotion and I understood that.

The subterranean sound of the petrels could be interpreted any way you liked: a love cry? a sound of bliss when the wanderer fed his mate and nestlings with oil? or the utterance of some emotion man cannot know?

The cries enchanted and mystified—unearthly, unreal, uncanny. What use were words? What was the meaning of the mad aerial dancing, anyway? Why did the birds not just come in from the sea, enter the burrows, and feed their mates? I was glad it was not my task to answer. This moment, this island, did not need to yield to interpretation.

The island no longer had any connection with the rest of the world. It had become a metaphysical chariot riding misty ether on its way to some astral place. We, the petrels and I, rode up with the island and soon their cries were calling at the edge of space.

The weird illusion sent me plunging through thickets, crawling among grasses and shoveling petrels aside. It sent me stumbling along the fringe of the forest where the flapping of birds tangled in the foliage sounded as if a thousand slaves sought to escape their bonds. It sent me down into a grove, its configuration suggested by the eerie glow of the mist. Against the contrast of tree and sky, I could see the petrels flitting like bats.

Eventually, I reached the ruins of an old puffin city. I sat there for an hour, the petrels no longer immediately overhead. Their voices sparkled in the distance, moving back and forth as if disembodied. The voices haunted, importuned: join the frolic! But once out of their presence, I chilled. It was cold and I had the choice of keeping on the move or leaving the petrels and going to sleep in my tent. I decided to keep moving.

I traversed the island in an hour of uncomfortable travel. There were no tracks. No one had ever lived on the island, so there had never been any traffic anywhere on it. Its occupants, apart from creeping mice (what did *they* live on? I wondered), were fliers, including the mosquitoes.

The mosquitoes attacked me the moment I stepped back into the forest. Countless generations of them had sucked nothing but the blood of petrels and I was the first man they had met, but they knew what to do with me. I have been bitten by mosquitoes in New Guinea and by black flies in the sub-arctic, but the mosquitoes of Gull Island have a special place in my memory. I tightened my collar and squashed them against my neck. They wriggled up my sleeves and down my spine, along with trickling runnels of water. They bit my back until it ran with blood.

The mosquitoes, rain and cold, the acute discomfort of bruised shins, twigs in my eyes, splinters gashing my hands, combined to discourage me. But I wanted to plumb the limits of the petrel's territory. There had to be an end to it. Branches whipped against my eyes; the petrels soared above me in an upended vault of sky. I remembered Marcel Proust's wonder at petrels (*he* called them sea swallows) and how their warmth in the surrounding earth reminded him of the satisfaction of being "shut in from the outer world." I remembered Alfred E. Gross, an ornithologist who studied petrels most of his life, and his wonder at them. "How can they survive, such frail birds, in the wastes of the sea? Very exciting and puzzling!" A biologist friend, Charles Huntington, his life devoted to petrel study, once told me, baffled, "How can I know so *little* about them?"

There were no answers as I struggled on, and I sought none. The cries rose and fell, sometimes quickened in urgent squawlings. The underground calls peaked in sudden emotion. Music ran through the earth.

I reached the end of the island. The petrels were as thick as ever. That meant they covered the entire island; that meant hundreds of thousands of them, perhaps more than a million, were concentrated on this one island from thousands of square miles of sea. Why this island?

I fumbled in a camera bag to see if the rain had penetrated it, and found a packet of matches. A fire would warm me, perhaps smoke out the mosquito hordes. I dug out dryish kindling from under the trees and piled up a big fire. It warmed me but it destroyed my night vision and the petrels were no longer wraiths of movement. Their cries lofted from the light of the fire. Then there was a rush of nearby sound; wings whined in the trees; cries noised at my ear, and a bird hovered over the fire. Another petrel darted down at the fire, turned sharply and knocked my hat off. A third struck me on the chest.

As I took my camera from the bag (a piquant thought: petrel pictures by campfire light), a fourth petrel dived into the fire, broke through a crust of red-hot wood, and entered the center of the holocaust. Before I could move, the bird was ablaze and the sharp stutter of its fiery wings sent blazing bits of wood flying everywhere. I reached forward; the crazed creature came out of the fire, a Catherine wheel of flames. It spun away, dropped into the grass and went out with a slow hiss. When I picked up the charred body, it was still pulsing with the last moments of life. A brown eye looked at me, saw, and closed.

I kicked the fire to pieces and sat down in the dark to await the return of my night vision. Wet now, exhausted now, cold now, imagination frozen now by the sudden destruction of the petrel, the rain a lamentation among the spruces, I wanted the night to end immedi-

ately. The petrels, like those marvelous free-falling gannets of St. Mary's, were unknowable and unreachable.

I shone the flashlight to see whether the mist was
thinning. As I swung around, I caught the reflection of
a jewel in the trees. I concentrated the beam. Two
jewels. I remembered Bill White telling me that two
years before, when the sea froze, a fox had walked across
the ice to the island. He must have been marooned, and
he watched now to see who was on his island. The
jewels vanished.

The sight of the fox was the final stroke of discour-
agement. Suddenly, I was chilled by the hostility of the
singing island. It attracted and it repelled. I was a part
of it, yet I must be driven from it, the mosquitoes seemed
to say, the cold and wet seemed to say, the terrible ter-
rain insisted; even the solitary fox told me to go. He was
being bitten by mosquitoes as well as I. He had to work
each night to catch petrels, not only to eat but to store
in the ground, enough to last him over the eight months
when the petrels left their island to hunt on the deep
sea between here and the coasts of Europe and Africa.

I could not bear the thought of life surviving against
such odds. Once, when betrayed by a great friend and
spurned by a wife, I had felt this helplessness at the
state of my world. How weak I was! How self-pitying
when I knew so well that the unstemmable urge of life
must have its way and that I must say yes to it.

I trudged along and the earth became silent as though
the petrels had retreated into the center of the island.

The flaunting cries were now at a great height, a majestic overtone to melancholy. Weeks before, they had seemed to say to me, on Kent Island, *Where, where, where-to-go?* Their cries no longer were a question. They affirmed the secret thought and spoke to me directly.

Go on, go on, go on there!

The cries thinned. Dawn was close. The first gull cry of the day growled deep in the mist. I trudged on and felt the illusion of the island waning with a delicious, slow-moving sense of release. The petrels were released, too, but in a more desperate equation: begone before the clock of light chimed the hour of the hunter.

Go on, go on, go on there!

The cries came from a great height and I felt the pull of the retreating birds and wept at their departure. Don't leave yet. I followed them up and away toward the open ocean.

One last cry, *Go on* . . .

I could see the shape of the mist in its passage over the island, and I saw the lights of Witless Bay in the west. A gull slid overhead, and I smelled honey in the growing light. The island was just an island again, asleep and no longer mysterious to day-borne man.

I could see down the cliffed and Cimmerian shore where the sea birds were awake and at work: puffins and gulls, murres and razorbills. But the island was not finished with me yet. I heard a sound in the grass near my glistening wet boots. I parted the grasses and a petrel looked up at me. She was caught, a twist of grass holding her firmly by one leg. Perhaps she had been on her way to relieve her mate in the burrow. Perhaps she had sought to escape and had been clutched at the last moment. Whatever had happened, she was desperate. I picked her up and she screamed, an astonishing sound from such a graceful creature. Now what to do? Release her to the mercy of the gulls, whom I could see in thousands offshore? Try to persuade her to re-enter the earth?

I introduced her to the mouth of every burrow nearby but she would have none of them. She wanted to be away to the deep sea where she belonged. Reluctantly, I let her go. In the next seconds, I got a startling insight into the way of another life. Such was her speed of flight, I almost lost her. She appeared for a moment as a big, almost falconlike, bird before me. Then her wings took hold and she jerked in front of a speeding puffin to begin a long, erratic, downward-moving flight toward several thousand puffins blanketing the water offshore.

At sea level, her speed did not diminish but she cut right and left over odd floating birds. Every movement of her body, from the moment of her release, showed acute concern. She did not want to be near the island which had drawn her so strongly at night. A terrible urgency drove her away.

Yet her terror seemed ill-founded. She flew close to scores of gulls but none of them paid her attention. Anyway, no matter where she flew, there would be gulls in her path. Now that she was flying so low and so surely,

I decided she was safe and well gone from the island. I glanced away for a moment, but my eyes were drawn back by an abrupt movement of gulls. The petrel, in one chilling second, had become the center of a death ritual.

She had been flying among herring gulls who were immature or only recently adult. Now, at water level, she was among adult gulls and the hunt was on. For a moment, I did not recognize the first attacker as a gull. His stiff wings and sudden deflections of flight made him look more like a bird of prey. He was quickly joined by his comrades, who formed two rings around the petrel. The outer ring circled, awaiting a chance to attack. The inner ring actively pursued the frantic petrel, who twisted, dived, doubled back. But everywhere she flew, the deadly sailplanes bore down on her.

The hunt was attritional. The petrel had speed and agility. In theory, she should easily elude a gull. But the gulls had their collective intelligence, which impelled them to keep forcing the petrel on the defensive. Only one of them might eat, but all must attack.

Within a minute, forty gulls were at the hunt. The brisk sea wind gave them a strange harmony of form and intent. They used the wind, acting on the topside of their wings, to drive themselves *downward* at the petrel. Their speed was so great that it was clear, despite the petrel's panicky turns and twists, that gull and petrel must collide eventually. The downward lunges, soaring rises, hoverings and bankings, made a grisly but beautiful ballet of flight. I wanted the petrel to escape, but my imagination was captured by the grace of the hunters.

The petrel was so well ringed by her enemies that to escape she would have to run among at least ten gulls in any direction she tried to break out. This seemed impossible; but the petrel was not concerned with possibility or reason. Never for a moment was there any relaxation of the thrust and parry of the hunt. All the creatures were absorbed.

The hunt moved over the heads of several thousand puffins who floated, unheeding, under the battle area. Puffins do not fear gulls, but suddenly, something alarmed them. Perhaps it was the intensity of the gull attacks; perhaps the petrel screamed her anguish. All the puffins took to the air at once. The water whitened as they thrashed into flight. I caught a brief glimpse of the petrel flying in the same direction as the puffins (perhaps she understood how she might escape). They rose around her and she disappeared into a loose-knit flock roaring away to the north. The gulls were merely gulls again, nothing menacing about them. Baffled, they hovered over the place where they had lost sight of their victim.

I kept my binoculars on the puffins and saw them spread out from their tight take-off pattern, and I saw, finally, a tiny shape twist away from their mass. She did not want to go north with them. Her destination lay to the south, on the Grand Banks, where she would be safe. She curved a hundred and eighty degrees back toward me now. Her flight with the puffins had taken her well away from her attackers and she was flying at high speed. She changed course slightly to avoid my island. Her only obstacles were a group of gulls resting on the water immediately opposite me. She changed course to miss them. Ahead lay Green Island with its bird hordes, including gulls. She deflected slightly to avoid that. Now, there was only the open sea, and with my glasses on her, she disappeared finally toward the distant banks.

The eastern light was brilliant though the horizon mist concealed the sun. Light glowed and flashed, seemed about to reveal itself but did not quite succeed. In the distance, columns of mist came out of the sea like upright giants, each one separate and distinct, having substance and a life of its own. I knew that the moment blue sky leaped into sight, the mist-giants would be destroyed. The sun would kill them.

Far distant, the hammering roar of Henry Yard's engine sounded. I sat down, overpoweringly tired.

At that moment, with a rush of regret, I knew that my visit to the islands was over, and that one day I must die.

ABOUT THE AUTHOR

Franklin russell is a Canadian citizen, presently living in the United States. He was born in 1926 in Christchurch, New Zealand, and received his education in that country and in Australia and England. From 1942 to 1948 he worked as a farmer, a contractor, an automobile mechanic, a laborer, truck driver, and streetcar conductor. In 1948 he became a newspaperman, working for papers in New Zealand, Australia, and Canada. He has been a contributor to magazines for many years and his articles, often illustrated with his own photographs, have appeared in such publications as *Maclean's, John Bull, Holiday,* and *Horizon.*

When not observing birds and animals or writing about them, Mr. Russell enjoys playing the harpsichord and studying Baroque music. He is currently working on a comprehensive natural history of the Gulf of St. Lawrence.

**RETURN THIS BOOK ON OR BEFORE THE
LAST DATE STAMPED BELOW**

MAY 9 1966	SEP 1 5 1977		
May 25	MAR 3 1 1978		
JUN 8 1966	OCT 27 1978		
JUN 2 4 1966	Nov. 13,'78		
	MAY 1 4 1982		
DEC 2 1 1966	AUG 3 1 1982		
JAN 3 1 1967	DEC 2 8 1985		
FEB 1 1 1967			
APR 1 4 1967			
MAY 3 1 1968			
OCT 2 1968			
JUL 1 '69			
MAR 22 '71			
APR 23 '73			

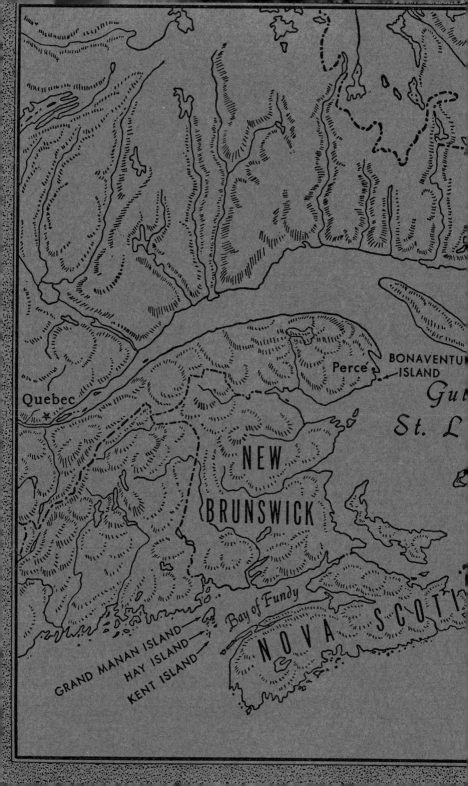